Winter's Thief

for dear Whess

Winter's Thief

Book 1

ANDEAN WHITE

Idea Creations Press
www.ideacreationspress.com

Idea Creations Press
www.ideacreationspress.com

Code for free maps: WT2014

Library of Congress Control Number: 2014951078

ISBN-13: 978-0-9888107-5-4
ISBN-10: 0988810751

Printed in the U.S.A.

Dedication

To Nancy, whose support and patience made this book possible.

Acknowledgements

There is a collage of family members and friends that participated in bringing this book to you. They reviewed the book, identified the confusing prose, redlined the early versions, and encouraged me to keep writing. I am ever grateful for their time, energy, and input.

However, it was Kathryn Elizabeth Jones, editor / coach / mentor, that found the pathway leading to the writer inside me. Her patience together with the occasional gentle nudge pushed me to drop the dang spy books and write this fantasy.

She knows her stuff. I had fun and learned more in four hours a month than in the first four years of spy short stories. I found a rich creative satisfaction as the writing principles began to control my thinking and presentation.

There is still much to learn, but I am confident Kathryn knows the way.

Also want to thank Nate Paret for his exceptional work on the cover. He took my vague description and turned it into art.

I wish to send a special thank you to Jeff Nish for loaning us his horse for the photo-shoot. Indy Grand is featured on the cover.

We could not have finished the photo-shoot without Kerry and Cody of Saltaire Barns. Thank you both for your excellent service and patience.

Winter's Thief

Part One

The Package

Oscar, trusted knight of the king, reduced the travel portion of his day to gather firewood and feed the tiny princess. A thin dusting of snow fell from the firewood as he whacked the pieces together. With the fire started, his strong hands squeezed the goat's milk into a small bucket. He lined a flute with silk purchased in Saraton, and continued to spoon milk from the bucket into the flute until the princess turned her head. She seemed to enjoy the milk. He placed a blanket across his square muscular shoulder and burped her.

Oscar did not sleep. The princess's day began with a diaper change, and another meal from the flute. His instincts were to press on and complete his assignment as quickly as possible. However, the small voice in his head and the princess's crying required him to slow his pace.

For two days he changed diapers, offered goat's milk through the flute, burped the baby, talked to her as if he were the same infant age, and fretted every minute about the baby's health.

On the last travel day, after the mid-day feeding, they were on the trail for twenty minutes when, from his right, a familiar eerie howl penetrated the still November air. He slowly ran his fingers through his short unkempt salt and pepper hair—the hereditary *aged* appearance was a benefit to the young Captain of the Long Bows.

Making the blanket into a sling, he placed the baby inside his coat. The long bow was removed over his head and the quiver positioned for quick access. A strip of the saddle blanket was used to tie the basket to the saddle.

Another howl from his left side pierced the air. A third howl from behind quickly followed.

His heart pumped rapidly. For the first time in six years, he had sweaty palms.

Oscar remembered the first time, when twelve, he'd watched a pack of wolves manipulate a doe. Three wolves had driven the doe into the silent waiting pack. After running for its life, it became the meal for nine adults and six pups.

He decided the safest direction was away from the pack ahead. He pulled an arrow from the quiver. Oscar held the bow and arrow in one hand. He untied the goat's rope, then tugged the reins to the right until the horse faced where they had just traversed.

The horse responded quickly to the kick in the hips. Galloping in the direction of the hopefully lone wolf at the rear, he continually scanned the trail.

Ahead, his silver eyes saw the fearless black wolf in the middle of the trail. Oscar tugged back on the reins and the horse stopped instantly.

Growling and baring its fangs, it crouched down on its front legs, making the horse shift nervously from side to side. Oscar stroked the horse's neck with his big hands as he repeated "Easy girl. Stand your ground." The horse, like the air, stood still.

Slowly, he aligned the arrow in the bow.

The wolf moved to its right and resumed growling and crouching. Oscar pulled the bow's string to his cheek waiting for the wolf to charge. Fully aware the other wolves would soon join this soldier guarding their escape, Oscar felt the time compressing. He decided he needed to take action. As he stood to release the arrow, the baby woke. From inside his coat the princess stretched and cooed.

The wolf backed up three paces and turned its head in confusion. When the baby began to cry, the wolf turned and ran off with its tail held high. Oscar heard the barking answered by the rest of the pack. The barking faded.

He turned back to the direction of the castle. Passing a puddle of fresh blood meant the goat was dead.

Without milk he needed to revise his plans. He stroked his square jaw covered with five days of beard stubble. Oscar could get milk at his farmhouse with eight hours of steady riding. His wife would be asleep by the time he arrived. He would milk the goat then move to the holding location near the castle.

* * *

The large boulders, strategically placed, hid the weathered grey oak half-door. This door had never been opened that Oscar could recall. Oscar grinned at the thought of the king's and queen's unawareness of the door, designed for the specific purpose of providing them a secret exit. If not for a chance meeting with the grounds keeper, Oscar would be entering the castle through the usual doors.

The baby snored and moved its tiny hands when he checked her in the sling. His attempts to reposition the sling ended in the baby having about the same space as the womb, regardless of his efforts.

The large key hung around his neck on a leather lanyard three inches below the baby. Carefully, he pulled his knife from the homemade scabbard. He protected the baby by placing his hand under her, and then positioned the knife to cut the strap. The key swung free from the right side and struck his left thigh. Gently he tugged the key. The lanyard slid around his neck until it fell to the ground.

To his surprise the key fit the keyhole and easily retracted the metallic rod without much effort or noise from either lock. But the corroded hinges appeared to be rusted into a solid mass of metal. Pulling on the door ring with all his strength finally dislodged the weathered door. Suddenly, the door stopped. Looking through the gap into the castle he found a rope tied to what appeared to be a coat hook. His knife wasn't long enough to reach. Unfortunately his sword hung on his horse grazing two hundred yards away. An arrowhead slowly cut the fibers as he sawed it against the thick rope.

It had been ten minutes since the two candles had passed the window at sunrise. He had only twenty minutes to make it to the queen's bedroom. The door finally opened enough for Oscar, of average height, to easily duck under the low header and enter the ... *closet?* Ten brooms, ten mops, ten buckets, and a tall stack of rags occupied more than half the room. Lightly knocking the wooden panels, the hollow sound informed Oscar which panel to move.

But someone had sealed the secret staircase. He replaced the panel then relocked the entry door.

The added weight of the baby tugged on the sling, making his neck sore. He rolled his head from shoulder to shoulder in both directions. The second time he stopped to check a movement in a window. The drapes were still swaying, but the person had disappeared. He walked to his horse, periodically checking the window.

After riding to the other side of the castle, he dismounted near the wagon side gate. Oscar walked the horse the final twenty feet and tied it to a tree.

Ten minutes left.

He took a deep breath before he entered the castle through the kitchen entrance. Inside the door, the hallway was dark but empty. The baby began to move, and Oscar could tell she was about to cry. He reached into his pocket for the feeding flute. The baby accepted the dry flute and fell back to sleep.

He walked fifteen feet into the forty-foot hall. Ahead, a sliver of light peeping from the kitchen door illuminated the hallway.

Laughter grew louder as the door opened. Hunter, the castle's assistant cook, placed a bucket of smelly kitchen waste in the hallway with two other buckets. Hunter turned to re-enter the kitchen. He stopped laughing as he came face-to-face with Oscar in the shadow of the door.

"Oh! ... Captain, good morning."

"Good morning, Hunter. How is your son?" *Would the pounding of his heart wake the baby?*

"We weren't sure for a few days," Hunter said. Then, a sly smile and short chuckle escaped his lips before he teased, "It's easier to sneak in through the stable door."

"Thanks, I will remember that next time."

An awkward moment hung in the air like the uncomfortable smell from the buckets. Oscar hoped Hunter would return to the kitchen so he could complete his mission. Every passing second increased the chance of exposure. *He was so close!*

"Well, I need to get back to work. Cheers, Oscar."

"Cheers."

Oscar wanted to rush up the spiral stairs, but nervously waited as his eyes adjusted to the limited light.

Ascending the stairs at the end of the hallway, he felt he would arrive at the queen's bedroom in time. Oscar thought about how he would convince his wife that Kendrick should have a sister if the baby wasn't needed.

The last danger waited at the top of the stairs—the thirty feet to the king's bedroom. The stairs ended at the large intersection of three hallways, each at least forty feet long with a full view of the king's bedroom door, and would be busy in another hour.

He heard footsteps on the lower stairs and voices from the right hallway. *They are going to catch me any second. Do I risk a dash across the opening, hoping no one sees me?*

The footsteps grew louder—close enough that Oscar could tell it was two people.

He would fake the king's greeting after knocking on the door.

Just as he was about to exit the stairwell, the voices disappeared with the closing of a door.

Oscar caught himself wringing his hands and biting his lower lip. To avoid detection, and because of his obsession to complete the mission, he had almost forgotten about the baby. Taking two stairs at a time had awakened her.

He knew from previous births that two chambermaids waited around the corner at the queen's bedroom door with water.

He reached in his coat to snuggle the baby in hopes of quieting her. The flute fell from under his coat and sounded like gravel under foot as it teeter-tottered end-to-end on the floor. Oscar picked it up and attempted to replace the flute, but the baby turned away.

Footsteps could be heard coming from the queen's hallway.

Quickly he tiptoed to the king's bedroom. As he closed the door, the two chambermaids rounded the corner.

The tip of his small finger could feel the baby feeding. A bead of sweat burned as it entered the corner of his eye. He placed his ear to the door.

"I thought I heard a baby cry."

"Me too."

"Probably an echo or something."

Oscar walked through to the private corridor leading to the queen's anteroom, and waited for the king's signal. He placed the baby in the bassinet and changed its diaper for a final time.

In the adjoining room, he heard the midwife's calming voice imparting instructions, the mother's efforts, and the king's encouragement. At times, everyone instructed, cried, or comforted in a birthing symphony.

"Push!" commanded the new midwife, who was willing to collaborate in the scheme as a matter of patriotic duty. And, as the superstitious king instructed, she was not part of the four stillbirths. She fulfilled Oscar's requirement to be strong willed and to manage the king if needed. And she was protected by her reputation in the village.

In the midst of the grumbling, groaning, and moaning that announced the arrival of a precious person, the faint two-knock signal filled the silent anteroom. Oscar removed the baby's diaper.

For a few moments, he heard the stillness of the castle.

And then suddenly, the door opened and the king's bearded square face revealed his solitary, somber countenance which informed Oscar another heir had died. Oscar took the still, tiny, male body from the king's large hands and placed it in the blanket that had previously carried the sleeping female baby. He gently placed the girl in the king's blanket. The tall king had to step back to show the baby to the midwife.

"It's a girl," she announced

The king pinched the baby's foot and the crying started.

Oscar felt a part of him had been taken when the door closed. He offered a quiet prayer for the soul he'd wrapped in the blanket. Oscar gathered the evidence of his stay in the anteroom and began the journey to bury the queen's still infant.

Halfway down the stairs he heard several people coming toward him.

"Do you have two goats now?" one voice said.

"Yes. My husband wants to breed them," replied another voice.

"Doesn't everyone already have a goat for the milk?" asked a third voice.

Oscar could hear water sloshing in buckets and brooms being lifted from stair to stair.

"That's what I said. Then he told me I didn't know anything about goats."

"How are you going to feed the goats that do not sell?"

Oscar wanted to hear the answer but decided he needed to retreat back to the king's bedroom. He reversed up the spiral stairs, traversed the intersection, and watched through the keyhole. Three maids carried brooms, mops, buckets of water, and rags. They chatted and giggled the length of the hallway.

Once quiet returned, Oscar quickly took the stairs to the bottom floor.

The empty, dark hallway invited him to enter, but he didn't want anyone to see him leave. He waited for another bucket of slop to be dropped in the hallway. Satisfied it was reasonably safe, Oscar walked toward the outer door. Three feet past the kitchen door, he heard the lock slide open.

He stepped behind the opening door and held his breath.

Another bucket of waste startled him when it was dropped on the floor. The door closed.

The sunshine between the oak door and the surrounding stone wall looked like a halo and provided a target at the end of the hallway. His eyes had to squint while he peered out the slightly opened door. Archbishop Thomas was walking in the middle of the street.

Sweat formed on his forehead.

Behind him, the kitchen door opened again. Another bucket dropped on the floor. The door closed.

Oscar felt trapped in the shrinking hallway.

Removing the tiny baby from the sling and gently laying it on the floor, he exited. Outside he watched the archbishop enter the cathedral—no one else in sight. He dashed back inside to place the body in the sling. Quickly he walked with determination to his horse.

An uneasy feeling came over him. He looked around and then rode off. Was he being watched?

* * *

The isolated location had been selected because it was exactly that—isolated. It wasn't near the four other graves or a road, farm, path, or trail.

Not wanting his horse to be tracked, Oscar tied it about a quarter mile from the site. The hood of his jacket protected him from the snow. He carried the shovel and the baby, and pushed through the thick bushes. He felt fortunate the cold mud wasn't frozen, refolded the baby blanket, and laid the tiny body in the unmarked three-foot grave.

He prayed.

The grave filled, Oscar had one more unpleasant command to complete. Like the delivery of the future princess, this task had a precise time element.

* * *Francine* * *

She awoke. The King's big hands gently stroked her chestnut hair from her small oval face while cooling her with a damp cloth.

"How is the baby?"

"She is beautiful," he said. He looked into her brown eyes.

"A girl! The throne could use a woman's view." The queen placed her petite shaking hands over closed eyes.

"She is very healthy, not like Daniel. Let me get her for you," the king said. He paused a moment. "Francine, my wife, our lovely daughter."

"You are so pretty," she said to the baby. "Have you given her a name?"

"I have not thought much about it. What do you think about Althea, your mother's name?"

"Althea would be nice." The queen looked at their heir, "Althea, what do you think?" The baby smiled. "I think Althea likes her name."

"Let me take Althea back to the bassinette. You get some rest."

The queen admitted the idea was good, but sleep evaded her. Instead, she thought about the depression experienced following the previous four boys' births. The last one, Daniel, had died after struggling to hold on to life for seven hours. If it had not been for Louis's intervention to force feed her water, applesauce, milk, and broth, Francine would still be talking with the dead. She was thankful her dream of raising the king's heirs would finally be fulfilled.

"Thank you," she said.

An unusual expression showed on the king's face before he said, "You are welcome."

Althea, a big baby compared to the boys, had good color.

Still, a nagging question occupied her mind as she fell asleep.

* * *Oscar* * *

Oscar arrived at the farmhouse mid-morning. He ordered the two Long Bows, who'd been protecting the mother, to go home. They had been gone for ten minutes when Oscar began to follow them.

As he rode, his thoughts were of the fading glamour of the Long Bows over the past five years. It began when

King Louis III had commanded Oscar to publicly execute three spies from Saraton. Oscar thought spying was a secret business and should be kept that way. Several times he had thought an argument with the king might have kept him from the *king's special assignments*.

The *old* king that Oscar admired would seek clever solutions and attempt to be fair in all decisions. The *new* king made decisions for speed to move along the agenda. Was Oscar's life and job merely defined as the king's henchman and baby carrier?

He rode a different trail to arrive at the last spot where the river and the road were close. The grassy flat area, the length of three wagons, next to the shoreline, was ideal for the task. The river curved deeply away. Should the bodies be found, they would be in an area far from the road.

He heard them talking. "I will be happy when we arrive at home. I want to continue my knight training. It's exciting to think of the intrigue, challenge, and the variety of assignments." The other one said, "I miss the training and camaraderie of the Long Bows, but I look forward to be assigned guard duty for one of the lords—better food, mostly inside, and predictable."

As he knelt he pushed an arrow into the soft soil along the inside of his left leg. Time's pace slowed as he aimed along the length of the arrow. He thought about his targets, their first three months of training, the practical jokes played on them, and their smiles when the king had knighted them.

A horse head appeared beyond the sharp edges of the rock outcropping, then the other horse head, followed by two young Long Bows riding high in the saddle. The phrase from his oath to the king echoed in his head, "...I will faithfully execute the commands of my king..."

He released the first arrow. The silent killer found its target. The other Long Bow whipped his bow over his head.

In a single, smooth motion Oscar's hand circled around to retrieve the arrow from the soil. The bow flexed its power as the string and arrow were pulled against his cheek. Oscar used the line of the shaft to find his target.

The young knight was retrieving an arrow from his quiver.

Oscar watched the flight of the arrow as the other silent killer found the remaining Long Bow's throat.

Oscar laid his long bow and quiver on the ground, pressed his hands together, and prayed for forgiveness.

The orange sunset enriched the red of the blood on the grass as Oscar dragged the bodies by their feet parallel to the river's edge. He made two rope harnesses and laid them on the ground next to the bodies. Pie-sized flagstones from the outcropping were laid on the harnesses and the bodies rolled on top of the stones. He laced a rope through the loops and pulled tightly.

New tears filled his eyes as he rolled the men into the river.

Their dried blood was left on the horses' sides. Invaders would be blamed for their deaths, theft of the saddles, and the stolen weapons he'd buried in a thicket of bushes. A surge from deep inside his stomach lifted to the top of his throat. It burned as he swallowed frequently to clear the pain. He dipped his head, swallowed one last time, and then said to his horse, "They were good men."

Oscar cleaned a few spots from his coat and then returned to the castle.

Family and Duty

Manshire province was the largest of three countries on the island continent. Crossing the forested country was a six-day ride from Saraton in the south to Worchestor in the north, and five-days from the ocean in the west to the vast eastern uninhabited mountainous region. The inevitable invasion of Saraton had ended eight months ago. The relationship with Worchestor was neither friendly, nor hostile.

Eight weeks after Althea's birth, she felt blessed to be the queen of Manshire. Stopping to look over the village each morning after breakfast had become a ritual. From her right she saw the perfectly shaped river and the dancing reflections of the morning sun as the river flowed by the stones in the manmade diversion. The defensive clearing beyond the river, covered with two inches of snow, was usually a large open field of transplanted ankle high grass with patches of white and orange wild flowers. The forest floor had been picked clean of all burnable firewood giving it a tidy appearance.

From her bedroom window, she saw the castle's wagon side gate, the kitchen utility entrance, the cathedral courtyard, and the hallway window of the cathedral's residence. Occasionally, the archbishop would wave, but not today. Through the sun's reflection, she attempted to follow his gaze. Was he staring at the four gravestones of her stillborn sons or enjoying the sunshine?

A yellow carriage and wagon stopped in the cathedral courtyard. James Smythe the Minister of Money Issues; Archbishop Thomas's father, along with Elizabeth his wife; and another woman the queen did not know, including a young girl, exited the carriage. The young girl was dressed in a yellow and white dress. Her coat, mittens, and hat were matching mahogany mink. Her long red hair had been gathered in a braid that draped in front of her left shoulder.

The librarian staring at the ground, held the doors open while the group entered the cathedral's library. A few minutes later, the librarian passed by the residence window without his coat, but wearing his hat. From conversations with the archbishop, Francine knew the librarian as a *hermit in the village*. He rarely talked of his life outside the library, and if he talked, it was usually about a book he'd read. The archbishop knew little about him other than he liked to read, was very reliable, and had a thin streak of grey in his otherwise black hair.

Ten minutes passed before the librarian returned with two men from the stable and unloaded a leather-monogrammed trunk from the wagon. The archbishop's visitors exited the library. The women, all except the young girl, hugged Archbishop Thomas. The unknown woman knelt, removed a medallion from her neck and placed it on the young girl. They hugged for an extended time until Thomas's father said something and circled his hands along his sides like he was gathering chickens. The women boarded the carriage.

Archbishop Thomas extended his hand to his father. A puff of steam exited his father's nose. He appeared annoyed that he had to remove his glove to shake Thomas's hand.

* * *

The queen entered the cathedral after a three-month absence. As she walked to her usual seat at the rear of the church, she noticed paint peeling on the columns, dirt marks from many hands, and unfinished floors. Dust had collected on every flat surface, and she smelled the first hint of a musty odor. Floorboards squeaked with every step. She dusted off the pew and sat.

The king controlled the money for cathedral repairs and it had been sparse for a couple of years. The queen's inquiries about the maintenance of the cathedral were answered by the king's disgust with the archbishop. Two years ago, he'd spent the window repair funds on a partial refurbishing of the rarely used cathedral's banquet room.

She closed her eyes and prayed.

The archbishop approached.

In her mind, she saw his small chin, large forehead, and receding hairline above his triangular face. She felt as if the archbishop was reading over her shoulder. A habit she detested.

"Good morning," the archbishop said. How are you today?"

"Amen." She finished, trying to ignore the interruption.

She heard his emphasized exhale, similar to the handshake she'd witnessed between Thomas and his father.

The queen had annoyed him; he had that emotionless blank stare waiting for her response. She opened her eyes. His face was like stone as he pulled on the collar that chafed his short neck.

"How are you today?" he persisted.

"I am enjoying motherhood. Althea has truly been a blessing."

"You have a kind heart and a willing spirit. I knew you would be a good mother. I can see it in the way you enjoy caring for the orphans." He turned his knees toward her.

She reached out to hold his big weak hands.

"That is why I stopped by today. Althea has a predictable schedule now, and I still wish to care for the orphan babies while you find them homes."

"That is good news."

"Did I see someone leaving a child three weeks ago?" she asked.

He acknowledged a passing parishioner before answering. "Yes, my younger sister left Bettina, her daughter. She is staying for some time while they are on holiday. You were spying," he added with a grin.

"Pretty name. How old is she?" The queen wondered about the size of the trunk but said nothing.

"Ten."

"If you need me to watch her for a while, I am happy to help," she said, grateful that she would provide a well needed woman's perspective, wondering at the same time if a young girl would interrupt his lifestyle.

"Thank you for the offer. I will keep that in mind. For now she is helping in the library as the librarian took a leave of absence for family matters. Hopefully, he returns soon, books are being misfiled and the priest is complaining about the extra duties."

"Are you teaching her?"

"I spend a couple hours with Bettina each day. She grasps concepts quickly and becomes bored with them just as quickly. Her artistic talent is exceptional, but often a dark destructive message comes forth in her work. I watched her for an hour a couple days ago. She drew a beautiful sketch of a farm, then modified the key elements of the sketch with flames coming out of the house, barn, and tallest trees."

* * Bettina * *

A week ago, the librarian had returned from his two-month leave of absence. Bettina could see the archbishop was happier that things were getting back to normal. The library was warm and lighted as they studied, and the books were returned to their proper location. Bettina was happy as she had a strange relationship with the librarian. They rarely talked, but worked together on a drawing for several sections of a candle clock.

Bettina had been with the archbishop for five months when the envelope arrived in the church's private postal couriers pouch. The librarian carried the envelope to the library where the archbishop was educating her.

"A letter from the diocese, your grace." His nerves appeared a bit jumpier this morning as he also handed the archbishop a letter opener.

"Thank you."

Archbishop Thomas slid the letter opener under the fold and ripped it through the crease. As Bettina leaned over him, her small hands rested on his rounded shoulders. Thomas opened the envelope. Inside was a water-stained letter from Mother. Carefully, he slid the letter opener through the second envelope.

He glanced at Bettina looking over his shoulder. Her dark eyes met his and then returned to reading the letter.

> *Thomas,*
>
> *It was good to see yo. .... left. I apology... ... ... imposition .. .. you. I hope ... ... Bettina can be.... .... friends, .. nee.. . .ood relationship now.*
>
> *. .rite to let you .... Father ... successful .. secur... ...m's release. Your siste. .. .appy to ....husband back.*
>
> *. will leave .... ..tter with the Operation Manager .. ... Smythe Family doc.. .... we*

reach Manshire. Father will sen. . .ouple servan.. .. fetch Bettina ... ..turn her to her home.

It seems .. .ad that Father ... . .o close to you, and we rarely talk. I wish Father was no. .. opposed to .... chose. ..ofession. I hope we can see you soon.
Love, Mother

He stared at the letter for a couple minutes before reading the other one. On official church stationary, the diocese letter read:

Archbishop Thomas Smythe:

We are saddened and regret to inform you that your father – James Smythe, mother – Elizabeth Smythe, sister – Rebecca Strenton, and her husband – Liam Strenton, did not survive the explosion onboard your family's ship bound for the Manshire Port.

The port master believes it was an accident based on stories collected from the seven survivors.

Please accept our deepest condolences. You and your family will be in our thoughts and prayers.

The enclosed letter was forwarded to us from the port master. It was found in the water after the explosion.

Archbishop Simon Fallstaff
Saint Sebastian Diocese

Uncle Thomas fell back into the chair. The note drifted to the floor.

"It was the king's fault," he said. "He started the war with Saraton that put the family on that dangerous ship. The king must pay!"

"When did this happen?" Bettina sniffed.

Archbishop Thomas looked for a date stamp. "Five weeks ago."

"We are not going to see them again, are we?"

"No. They are gone."

"What is going to happen to me?" Bettina asked. Her cheeks felt hot and her heart pounded as if it was going to leap from her chest.

"You will stay here...with me," Thomas replied

Bettina noticed his pause and wondered what he didn't say.

"We will find you some friends," Thomas continued.

"Like who?"

"Well the queen for one. She likes you."

"She does not."

The archbishop breathed heavily. "Well, perhaps..."

In the end, Bettina realized that her life was a mess, and then some. Not only did she have to live with her cruel uncle, she had no parties to attend and no new ball gowns to put on. Plus, there were no servants here, and she liked servants—they catered to her, helped her—and now life would remain ruined for all time.

* * *Oscar* * *

Oscar's house was a typical pole frame structure with white plaster siding and the annual fresh grass roof. Inside, the stone and mortar fireplace was the central structure. It served as the roof support and had a pot handler frame that Oscar had traded for archery lessons with the blacksmith. Two shutter covered windows, one on each sidewall, were opened on warm days and closed on cold. Burlap sacks were stuffed in the openings in winter.

The one big room had a handmade eating table with four chairs by the window in the first corner, and the larger bed in next corner. The adjacent corner had a smaller bed and the last corner was the kitchen area with a smaller table and a water bucket, which rested under the other window, along with Abbey's prized possession— a cast iron kettle, a gift received from *her two boys* designed to help her deal with her progressive disease. Kendrick's smile alternated with a *this is heavy* frown as he carried the kettle to Mother.

Cleaning the kettle after a dinner of wild pig stew, Oscar said, "Abby, I want to take Kendrick to the village to buy seeds and gather some stones for the irrigation system. I think the Hamiltons will let us use their new horse drawn wagon."

"This would be a good time to teach Kendrick how to drive a wagon," she answered as she limped outside. "They have done well for themselves the past few years."

* * *

The following morning, Kendrick rode behind his father on Oscar's horse to the Hamiltons. Both were quiet on the ride there.

The Hamiltons were happy to loan their horse and wagon. And it was a special treat. Kendrick had never seen a new wagon. The oak bed and bench seat were a honey color oak. Two wheels and harness tongues were the only things jutting out from the big box. Reginald helped them harness the horse to the wagon, and Oscar's horse was tethered to the rear.

Kendrick unbuckled then re-buckled the harness as Reginald showed how the harness was assembled—his brown eyes darting between his hands and Reginald's. After the last buckle was secured, a thin but strong

Kendrick jumped onto the seat, grabbed the reins, and called to Father that it was time to go. Oscar sat in the remaining seat on the wagon, ruffled his son's short brown hair, took the reins as he told Kendrick to relax, and instructed him to watch how the horse responded to his hands. They waived to Reginald and the twins as Oscar slapped the reins.

"If the reins are evenly distributed side to side the horse goes straight," he said. "It's like they float on water." Kendrick's large eyes watched his father gently lift the reins on one side and tug on the other. And sure enough the horse moved with the tug, like a boat's rudder. A sharper turn required a longer tug. A gentle slap of either rein increased the horse's speed; to run required a slap of both reins.

Kendrick's focus became concentrated and finally Oscar asked, "What are you staring at?"

"You are so calm, and this is easy for you to do. Will I ever master this skill?"

"Yes, son. And, maybe better."

Finally he gave the reins to Kendrick who drove the last couple of miles to the farm supply warehouse. His excitement was quite evident. Oscar felt proud, that was until Kendrick cut a corner too close. The wagon fell into the four-inch deep ruts, but it felt like several feet as it jarred to a stop. Kendrick stiffened and over reacted trying to manage the horse for a gentle exit from the ruts. Momentarily both wheels were back at ground level before the right wheel dropped into the left rut.

"Relax, Kendrick. Let the horse do the work," his father said.

Kendrick gently pulled the right rein, and the horse pulled the wagon back to level. The rest of the trip was uneventful.

Oscar took his horse to the barn, showed him how to care for the Hamilton's horse, and checked the wagon for problems.

That night at dinner, Kendrick told his mother, "I made the horse turn right and left by tugging the reigns." His hand bumped the water cup.

"Careful Kendrick," Oscar said.

"Then, the horse put us in the ruts. I had to drive us out," Kendrick continued.

Oscar smiled at Abbey.

"Oh, I forgot. Reginald showed me how to harness the horse to the wagon." Kendrick was quiet for a few moments. His eyes opened wider and his head tilted up. "Can we get a wagon? I could do more around the farm? We need to have a horse too. I would take care of it."

Extended Family

A day had passed since the queen had received the archbishop's request to meet him mid-morning at the cathedral. She'd handed her response to the librarian, who'd entered the castle through the kitchen utility door. She'd smelled the slimy stench of the leaking buckets from the hallway.

She assumed the archbishop wanted to talk about Bettina. He and his charge had had a couple of loud arguments the past three weeks and the queen guessed he was going to ask if Bettina could stay in the castle.

He had told her once, in a rare moment of weakness, that a deciding factor for becoming an archbishop was he would not have children. He didn't want anyone to have to face a similar, awful childhood.

When Queen Francine entered the cathedral, she sat in her usual place on the last pew. Waiting, she again noticed the cracked paint like a dry pond in autumn and some flakes rolling at the edge. The entry floorboards were loose and most squeaked from rubbing on the loose nails. The lacquer had worn from the edges of the pews.

She heard his slippers tapping on the marble floor even before she saw him.

"Good morning Queen Francine."

"Good morning, Archbishop."

"We have not had any abandoned babies lately," the archbishop said.

"Hopefully, that's a sign the times are good as people can care for their babies. The king must be making good decisions."

"Maybe so," he said. His gaze left her eyes to somewhere above her head.

"What is so important to send the librarian with the note to wait for an answer?"

"I have a favor to ask."

She turned to face him and noticed his slumping shoulders. The archbishop drummed his fingers on the edge of the pew.

"What is it you want to ask?" she began.

"Bettina is depressed and moody. The harder I try, the worse she gets. She has an exceptional art skill that is being wasted by her attraction for destructive forces. In her latest drawing I could imagine the colors in shades of grey drawn with charcoal and felt the breeze from the drawing touching my cheeks. I felt the confidence of the old farmer herding his sheep toward the meadow and could smell the dust swirling as they walked out of the corral. This sketch, one of four unaltered by the flames, rockslides, lightning, and...floods destroying the landscapes, farmhouses, and animals that were so...disturbing in the other sixteen drawings—her drawing focus seems to be getting...worse...especially since the letter from the diocese."

The archbishop paused for a few moments—his eyes moving about as he cleared his throat twice.

"I think she needs a mother. I really do not want to ask, but I cannot help her anymore. Would you consider taking her in for a couple of months to see if you can help her?"

"I would be happy to help if I can," she said, though it would be the oldest child she'd helped.

"Will the King mind?"

"I will worry about the King," she said, thinking of the unsolved problems between Louis and Thomas.

"Let me inform her. Can you be ready in two days?"
"Yes."

* * *

Queen Francine brushed three-year-old princess Althea's blonde hair.

"You have pretty hair." She paused, waiting for a response. "Althea, when someone compliments you, you should say 'thank you'."

Althea's eyes alternated between her mother's and her own hair.

"Thank you. Why is my hair not dark like yours?"

"It happens once in a while," she said. "It might change when you get older." Her heart stopped briefly, recalling the struggle she'd had with that very same question. *My mother had an aunt with light sandy hair.*

"What are we doing tomorrow?" the princess asked.

"Tomorrow brings your first trip to the market. We will go before lunch to avoid the large crowds."

"What is the market?"

"It is an exciting place where people buy and sell items of value. You will like it. Come, it is time for bed."

Althea knelt by the bed and quietly mouthed the words of her prayer. She jumped into bed. The queen pulled the covers up under Althea's chin and kissed her on the forehead. "Good night, Althea."

"Good night, mother."

By mid-morning the queen, Althea, and three Long Bows were ready for the market. Althea's excitement bubbled over like unattended boiling water. Her new shoes pattered on the brick street as she ran ahead to the next gate and reported back to the queen.

"This is so exciting!"

The queen knelt to talk to Althea. "While we are in the market area, you cannot be running around—you will get lost. Promise me, you will hold my hand or dress."

"I promise." She rolled her lower lip and displayed her best sad eyes.

"Althea, a princess should not do that in public!"

After ten minutes, Althea appeared bored. She released the queen's dress. In an instant, she was lifted onto the bodyguard's shoulders.

"This is fun," she clapped, looking, pointing, and smiling at every activity. She touched the flags on the carts, pointed at the carts selling toys, and swung her head from side to side. She clapped for the juggler. The bodyguard held her feet as she bounced on his shoulders.

At one of the children's clothing carts, a young woman held two pink dresses.

"Are you going to buy them both?" the queen asked.

"I have twins. I am looking to see what else is available in pairs."

The cart's tattered canopy must have blocked her vision until the bodyguard moved to his left, because suddenly, the young woman's vivid blue eyes stared at Althea, seeming to take in every inch of her. The woman brushed her light sandy hair from her eyes, still staring at the princess.

Suddenly, all color drained from the woman's face and Francine noticed the distinct trembling of her hands as the woman handed her the two dresses. "Forgive me," she said, "but I guess I will not be needing them after all."

With the lovely dresses in Francine's arms, the woman walked away.

* * *Bettina* * *

From the time of her arrival, the dining room had been under construction. At present, the general room needed soft pastel green paint and gold trim. The ceiling mural of angels taking children to heaven was still in need of restoration. The wall mural of Moses crossing the Red Sea was complete.

On the right side of the table were four access doors, which had not been used in more than five-years, but were completely refurbished.

The like *new,* thirty-year-old, banquet table and padded chairs, could seat thirty people. Tonight, it was just two.

Archbishop Thomas and Bettina's dinner together had become a time of quiet and eating and not much else. She questioned—no believed that—his ability to raise her was completely inadequate. It felt as everything he tried fueled her anger. A couple of flare-ups turned into bonfires and had actually appeared to frighten him.

"Bettina, I apologize for the fate of your life and my inability to communicate with you," he began. "With your consent, I would like to have you spend some time with the queen. My hope is she can guide you in ways that benefit you."

"No!"

"No, what?"

"No, you do not have my consent," she said.

"May I ask why?" Thomas put his utensils on his plate, pushed his plate back, and leaned on his hands.

"No." She continued to eat.

"So you would rather be bored most of the day here, than take a chance on something new? You would avoid a chance to find out who you are?"

"No."

She had placed her utensils on the dish and crossed her arms.

"Bettina, you are very bright. You could have a promising future." He cleared his throat. "If I could wish anything for you, it would be to use this opportunity to enrich your life." He looked away to his left.

"Thank you for dinner." She stood and left the table.

* * *Francine* * *

"How did your visit with Bettina go?" the queen asked.

"Not well. I wish I could get a glimpse of what she wants. I would give that to her."

"Do you want me to order it done? I am the queen."

"No. Let me try to convince her."

Bettina appeared. The library door had not squeaked; they had not heard her footsteps. She wore traveling clothes similar to when she'd arrived, with the family medallion around her neck. Her recently shortened red hair and a devilish smile had caught the queen's attention.

"Bettina, as you know, I have grown...concerned about...my ability to raise you. And as we discussed, I would...like for you to spend a...few months with the queen." His usual confident voice betrayed him. He paused.

"I have also thought this over, and agree to this *test*," Bettina said. "I have become bored here. A change will be helpful."

"Really?"

"I am growing-up."

"How old are you?" the queen asked.

"Twelve."

"I see," the queen said. She nodded to the archbishop. "Are you prepared to move into the castle?"

"Yes. Let me get my coat and hat. I left them behind the first book shelf."

He appeared to suppress a smile that appeared momentarily on his face. A bounce in his step gave his truest feelings away as he left them.

The solid oak desk was more like a table. The two drawers on either side were still functional with some physical effort. It had served two crowns until King Louis III had had another desk made to fit his tall body. It was the anchor piece in the large, windowless office. A desk chair, visitor's chair, double wide four-shelf bookcase, and a wool rug made up the other office furniture.

The queen opened the door and lit the oil lamp.

"Come in. Bettina, we are happy to have you here. This is my meeting room where I conduct the queen's work. For that purpose, it isn't often used, but it needs to be cleaned and organized so people will respect my authority. You may use it for your drawings, but you cannot draw anything outside of what you find in these books. I would like for you to keep the room cleaned and organized. Let me show you how I like it."

"Yes, ma'am."

"You may call me Francine in private, but you should use 'my Queen' in public."

"Very well."

The queen explained how to file, organize the books and desk, and accomplish some general housekeeping duties.

"Let me escort you to the maids' quarters. They have prepared a bed and carried your storage trunk there. I thought it would be better to be with women closer to your age. I guess the accommodations are below your expectations, but you will have someone to talk to. You should show them some of your art this evening."

Bettina was silent. She bit her lower lip and tilted her head slightly, then instantly gave a smile.

"I shall try."

"That is what I had hoped for."

* * *Oscar* * *

Abbey held the egg between her rigid hands as she cracked it against the side of the bowl. The egg fell from her grasp to the floor. The slow oozing of the egg white and yolk followed the muffled smack.

Oscar carried the pot to the fireplace—Kendrick cleaned up the egg.

"Are you all right?" Oscar asked. "Do you need us to do anything before we leave?"

She straightened her back and lifted her face.

"No. No. I will be fine," she said.

"We should be a few hours." He kissed her, thinking of her strong spirit and positive attitude throughout her affliction. After latching the door, he stared at the ground for a few seconds and smiled as he thought about Abbey.

Before the loss of her hand's flexibility, she'd left notes in his hatband encouraging him to be careful, to be alert, or to come home. He had kept the notes in his barracks locker. Today's breakfast reminded him of every Saturday morning when Abbey had made his favorite omelet. Each Friday during blooming season he brought her a bouquet of wild flowers. On Sundays, they enjoyed biscuits and gravy made from Oscar's special recipe. During harvest, they worked side by side—the work was hard but their devotion was strengthened by their shared accomplishments.

Their love continued to grow with Kendrick's birth. They talked about all the opportunities they would provide for their son—education, a strong moral character, farming skills as he grew, a plot of land at seventeen and a home when married.

During a seven-month period and when Kendrick turned three, Oscar was promoted to Captain of the Long Bows, and Abbey's joints began to stiffen and swell. The demands of Oscar's job advancement, and the advancement of Abbey's immobility had brought an end to the thoughtful gifts, but not their love.

He lifted his head, saw Kendrick waiting, walked to the wagon, and mounted his horse. They were past the curve as Oscar rode alongside Kendrick.

"Take your time. I am going to ride ahead to talk with Reginald. Remember, Reginald has entrusted us with the wagon, and we need to care for it. On the way back, I will let you control the horse. See you in about twenty minutes."

Thirty minutes later Kendrick arrived at the Hamiltons. Oscar and Reginald were sitting on two large cut logs talking and watching the twins play. Reginald was the first to stand and walk toward the wagon.

"Welcome Kendrick. How was the wagon?"

"Very good. No problems."

"I hear you are an excellent driver."

"Yes. I am." Oscar and Reginald laughed.

"Kendrick, we should return home," Oscar said. He sat behind the saddle.

On the ride home, Oscar told Kendrick stories about growing up and his early days in the Long Bows, including one about an early encounter with the archbishop when he suddenly stopped talking.

It was the sound he heard first, a sort of sobbing plea that made him ache inside.

He reached around his son, grabbed the reins, and kicked the horse. When they were beside the gate, he pulled the reins taut. The horse stopped. Kendrick slid off the saddle. Oscar rushed to Abbey's side.

"What is it, Abbey?" He rubbed the dirt from his hands onto his shirt then wiped her tears.

"I cannot pick up any of the potatoes or pull the carrots."

Oscar cupped her face in his hands and stared into her eyes as he continued to wipe the tears with his thumbs.

"You will be like new in a few days. We should get you into the house."

He carried her through the garden's gate, across the grass, and toward the house.

Birthday Surprises

The queen and her daughter, dressed in matching light blue dresses, sweaters, and hats, attracted more attention than usual. A special occasion required special memories, which is why Queen Francine had proceeded with her shopping excursion even after she'd discovered two of the three assigned Long Bows were sick.

The air was full of noise—minstrels performing, babies crying, children playing, people clapping for magicians, cart owners peddling, and dogs barking. Brightly colored handmade flags were hoisted above the carts to attract attention. It was an exceptionally busy market.

The lone, third bodyguard's blank stare was temporarily replaced with a forced smile when he interacted with the queen or Althea. So far, she had purchased a book and a doll for Althea's birthday.

At each cart, the bodyguard set the bag down and lifted Althea onto a box or barrel so she might see above the carts. Each time, Althea said, "Thank you." She appeared not to miss anything—the crowd, the minstrels, the jugglers, boys teasing girls, children chasing, customers buying, merchants selling, and three men huddled together at the fountain where the three streets intersected.

A woman bumped into the bodyguard. The queen noticed but did not think much about it until she noticed the woman staring at Althea. She started to say something to the bodyguard, but the woman moved on.

It took a few minutes to find the right size and color of rabbit fur gloves for Althea. A broad shouldered man wearing several grey shirts moved through the crowd. He was shorter than most men, but had a muscular build. The queen watched him as he stopped and talked a few carts away.

She paid the merchant. The new items were added to the bag. Althea jumped off the box. The queen held Althea's hand. Their small caravan proceeded to another cart of children's toys where the queen hoped to find a memory game.

* * *Oscar* * *

Oscar entered the barracks to find two Long Bow's sleeping in their bunks.

"Get out of bed."

They opened their eyes, and appeared to struggle sitting up.

"Who took your place on the queen's shopping detail?"

"Captain, we are truly sick. The queen did not wait for us to find replacements."

"Did you follow–up after she left?"

"No, sir."

"How long ago?"

"Uh, three quarters of an hour?"

"What were they wearing?"

"Light blue dress and hat—both of them."

"Find replacements *now*, or pack your stuff and leave!"

"Yes, sir!"

Oscar ran through the barracks, knocked over a mop bucket, ran up the castle street, and exited the side gate. He stopped. From his position he saw three quarters of the crowd.

There she is!

The man wearing several grey shirts had just bumped into the queen. The man pushed the single bodyguard backwards. The bodyguard swung his arms like a windmill trying to keep his balance but fell. A second man grabbed Althea. He ran carrying Althea as she screamed for her mother. The grey shirted kidnapper led the way through the crowd.

Althea was taken in seconds from a crowded market. Her loud high-pitched scream pierced the air. Several men attempted to stop the abduction, but they were bowled over by the grey shirted kidnapper.

Oscar was already running. He was ten-horse lengths from the two kidnappers when a third man tackled him from the side.

Oscar rolled then stood up. He took two steps toward his tackler and punched him on the jaw. When the tackler threw his counter punch, Oscar leaned back and felt the air on his face as the fist grazed his nose. A gentle push of the attacker's fist exposed his back and Oscar punched him on the lowest rib. The attacker groaned then turned to face Oscar. Before he set his feet, Oscar struck him above the heart. The attacker fell to his knees then fell face first onto the cobblestones.

"Tie him up," he instructed the surrounding merchants.

Oscar looked over the crowd. Althea's light blue hat exited the market area. He yelled, "Out of the way!" and pointed at the hat. The crowd opened a path for Oscar to run through.

The kidnappers were over ten lengths ahead.

Oscar pulled an arrow from the quiver. Running full speed with the arrow in one hand and his bow in the other, he was determined to catch up.

He was surprised that the grey shirted kidnapper turned to fight him.

Oscar placed the arrow in the bow, pulled the string to his cheek, and leapt in the air to steady the bow. The arrow entered the right shoulder of the surprised man. As Oscar passed, he struck the kidnapper's temple with his right elbow and retrieved the arrow with his left hand. The kidnapper fell to the dirt.

Althea's thrashing arms and additional weight hampered the speed of the last kidnapper. In a few seconds, Oscar was two-lengths behind him.

The kidnapper turned and threw Althea at him. He caught her, planting his feet, but slid wildly on the dirt. Stumbling over a tree root, he landed on the ground.

"I apologize princess," he said.

Placing her on the ground, he jumped to his feet. He turned toward the escaping kidnapper who was four-lengths away running through the trees. He released the arrow. The kidnapper moved to the right to avoid the tree where the arrow stuck.

"Flaming dragons!" Oscar cried. He wanted desperately to chase the abductor, but knew his rightful place was protecting the princess.

She was standing and brushing off her clothes when Oscar returned.

"I am sorry, princess," he said. Oscar dusted his clothes.

"Thank you. I am all right."

He was surprised by her answer. She appeared calm and casual about the affair.

"We should get you back to the castle."

She reached and held his hand. "Mother said I should hold hands while in the market." They walked in the loose dirt outside of the market area.

The grey shirted kidnapper had disappeared. A small bloodstain dyed the dirt where he had fallen.

Just then he saw the queen, holding her dress above her calves, walking quickly through the forest of people. Her face was flushed, and her breathing was labored. They met at the end of the cobblestone street. She knelt and hugged her daughter. "How are you?"

"I am well."

The queen stood and started to lean in toward Oscar, but stopped.

"Thank you!" the queen said.

"You are welcome, my queen."

The cheering crowd was loud. The market crowd parted slowly as the three walked toward the castle. Oscar's anxious pace quickened and he looked to the queen for cooperation. She stared into his eyes and shook her head slightly.

Oscar received several pats on the back. He talked with the men who attempted to stop the abduction, and thanked them. The queen nodded in approval.

She continued on through the castle gate.

Oscar stopped at the third kidnapper being guarded by the two sick Long Bows.

"Take him to the jail. I shall interrogate him shortly."

They gripped his arms and forced him to stand. Oscar blinked only once before walking away. Just then a whispered whoosh of an arrow stopped dead in the kidnapper's heart, missing Oscar by only inches.

* * *Bettina* * *

The winds were strong. Leaves were trapped and blowing around in small eddies at corners where they'd lost contact with the wind.

Bettina watched as Hunter checked the paper he'd found under a couple of stones. His index finger nodded up and down seven times as he counted off the boxes. He scratched his head, then shrugged his shoulders and carried the first box in through the kitchen utility entrance. Hunter had one case left to haul inside when Bettina walked away from the window.

She checked under her bed to be sure the case of tea, special ordered by Uncle Thomas, was hidden.

* * *Oscar* * *

From his barrack window, Oscar watched the chambermaid run across the courtyard to get out of the first biting wind of the cold season. Long blades of the decorative grasses whipped about. The envelope she carried nearly blew from her hand, twice.

She knocked on the captain's door, presented the invitation, and curtsied, then returned to her duties.

Oscar slid his knife along the flap's crease.

> *Oscar,*
> *Althea has asked that I send you this invitation to her birthday party this Saturday. If the king's duties permit, you may join us for lunch, but please join us for refreshments after. Thank you for making this day possible.*
> *Eternally Grateful,*
> *Francine*

* * *Francine* * *

On the day of the party, the assembly hall had been converted to the princess's party room. Decorations of ponies and brightly colored flags crafted by the staff were sewn onto the curtains, placed on tables, and draped over the chandeliers. A couple of tubs filled with water to bob for apples and tables for blocks were set up on either side of the long lunch table and centered in the room. To one side, a table was set for the king and queen, and other adults. A few minutes before noon, children entered the room to take seats at the lunch table. Ten minutes past noon, Althea entered the room to the cheers of the children. The king and queen followed and walked to their table.

Venison pasty with potatoes, and applesauce, Althea's favorite foods—were served.

Oscar arrived as the tables were cleared. Bettina sat by the queen. The archbishop and others had been invited by protocol.

One hundred pastries outlining a large "5" were wheeled in on a cart. Several partiers could be heard gasping their ooh's and ahh's.

While the children ate, the adults were busy talking about the queen's recent pregnancy.

The king looked at Oscar. He raised his dessert and gave a single nod that implied, *Thank you.* Oscar raised his pastry and returned the nod. Someone was tugging at his shirt.

Althea.

Turning in his chair he said, "Happy Birthday Althea. What can I do for you?"

She kissed him on the cheek. He watched her run to her friends as he touched his cheek.

ANDEAN WHITE

Early Manhood

Abbey's physical condition continued its gradual decline. Occasionally, she would tell her husband, "Each day my memory of what it feels like to be normal slips further away." Her stiff joints kept her in bed two mornings a week. The knots on her knuckles were the size of grapes, making the simple tasks difficult. Her index and middle fingers had the same shape as the glass on the castle's oil lamps. The third and little fingers were beginning to have that same look. The immobility of her fingers had made her hands rigid like a garden spade. Scooping autumn potatoes created even more scars, scars that eventually callused the heels of her hands.

Her willpower and pride had carried the family. She had collected the traps set by Oscar, reset the traps when Oscar was on long assignments, tended the garden, hauled water, and cooked. On trying days after the extreme pain threatened to stop her, she would soak her hands and feet in hot water and then return to work. She knew in the future she would no longer be able to care for herself, or Kendrick.

Kendrick stayed close to help as needed. Manhood would find him too early. She reasoned the family needed him to be responsible for food, the garden, the repair of the house, and her own personal care.

Kendrick's role in the family had been discussed with her husband. Though opinions changed with each conversation, they both knew a change in their routines was forthcoming.

* * *Kendrick* * *

After a pheasant and bread dinner, they gathered at the handmade eating table—a wedding gift from Oscar's parents. The top was a three-inch flat slab from a forty inch oak tree. Oscar's Father was the first to build tables with leg space created by a center support post. The four oak chairs each had a suspended weaved leather seat.

Abbey wiped the table while Oscar brought in some firewood. They waited for Kendrick to finish the dishes.

"Kendrick, we need to discuss you taking on more responsibility," Oscar said. "First, we need to train you in trapping, hunting, and fishing. Come with me tomorrow morning so you know where the traps are, and we will set new ones. Your mother can teach you to do the tasks around the farm."

The next morning, he and his father loaded the handcart with four empty traps. He showed Kendrick the locations of the traps, how to use wooden wedges to find the next trap, how to prepare the trap, and how to select trap locations. He let him set some of the traps.

A few of the traps had snared birds, squirrels, or rabbits. Kendrick learned to prepare the animals and birds for supper.

At the farm, Oscar gave his son archery lessons.

Kendrick and his mother survived the first week with a few mistakes. One bird escaped the trap when the door was left open. He'd spent half a day looking for the goat he'd forgotten to put in the barn the night before. Kendrick's red forearm was tender from the bowstring striking it.

On bad days, his mother would watch him from a chair near the house door. On good days, she'd trim the rose bushes, garden the window pots, and tend the garden. In the evenings she'd teach him the alphabet, how to read, and how to solve basic math problems.

His father would arrive mid-afternoon on Fridays and immediately begin working on tasks Kendrick was too small for. Their Saturdays were similar to two farmers working to bring in the harvest—work from sun up to sun down, with little rest, but great satisfaction.

Frequently Kendrick's internal smile showed on his face as a strong bond developed between them. He was happy to exchange hard work for Father's winks, smiles, and kind words. On Sunday mornings his father would discuss the importance of education, loyalty, integrity, finishing anything started, and friends. Once a month he'd spend time developing survival skills in archery, knife throwing, fishing, etc.

Sunday afternoons happened to be family time. He read stories to his parents, Mother talked of growing up with four sisters and one brother, and Father told stories of youthful adventures. Occasionally, they would tell stories of dragon legends, mystical magicians, fearless knights, and witches.

Two particular Sunday afternoons stood out.

The first had to do with the feelings of his parents:

"Kendrick, you are doing a wonderful job around the farm. Your mother and I want to give you a knife and this leather for the scabbard to show our gratitude. We are so blessed to have a marvelous son like you. Thank you."

The second remembrance was in the telling of a prank he and King Louis III had played on the now Archbishop Thomas.

"Thomas was our age, eleven, when his family moved into the castle," his father began. "We played in the Camel Humps. After a while his older sister, Regina, would retrieve him for math, art, and music lessons. We decided to give him a free afternoon by taking him camping. We met, hiked to the pond on the west end of the marsh, and taught him to fish, skip rocks, and cook. He entertained us with one of his plays.

"When Thomas went to sleep early, we built a raft. We placed him on the raft and pushed it into the pond. He woke in the middle of the pond. But he had a fear of water. He screamed like a wolf finding his pack and called us all sorts of names, which I'd rather not mention, but we just laughed. He got angry and paddled in a circle.

"The king, a child then, told Thomas the water was only knee deep. So when Thomas had enough courage to step off the raft, the water was actually waist deep, precipitating another round of name-calling. He waded slowly toward shore, holding on to the raft, like a lost puppy."

"That day, he swore revenge on both of us."

"Father, how did Thomas end up back here?" he asked.

"At fourteen, Thomas left the castle for advanced education. His new home was across the street at the cathedral. Thomas's basic theology education was followed by three years as a vicar, and two years at the diocese. He returned to Manshire as a priest. Thomas was appointed archbishop after two years of service to the previous archbishop. I suspect his family's wealth and donations played a part in his rapid advances and location choices."

"Where did the previous archbishop go?"

His father hadn't answered him. He stared out the window in silence for half a minute and then turned back to Kendrick.

"It's time to rest. Time to go to bed."

Red Scarf

Althea enjoyed their trips to the market. The queen assumed this was because it was the opposite of castle life. So much activity concentrated in three intersecting streets kept her busy. She tried to hear every conversation, watch every transaction, and enjoy the colorful surroundings. Unfortunately, after the kidnapping attempt, an adult was always holding her daughter's hand, and the knights had been increased from three to five, two of which were dressed like the crowd.

On this trip, the queen gave her extra attention as she explained how to select goods.

"Here is a material cart. Today, we are looking for linen to make the baby a bed shirt." She rubbed her hand over her belly. "If they have enough material, we will make you a new dress, too."

"Mother can I pick the color?"

"Yes you *may.*"

"Mother, *may* I pick the color?"

"Perfect. Yes."

"This is wool. Feel the rough texture. It's used for making warm clothes to resist the cold," she explained. She returned the wool sample and picked a cotton sample.

"This is cotton. It feels durable. Work clothes are made from cotton. It is available in a variety of colors. Lighter colors are best for outdoor use."

"This last sample is linen. It is a lighter material and looks nice for proper occasions and wedding dresses. Feel how light this is. This yellow would make a nice spring dress."

Althea rubbed the cotton and linen samples. "This is so smooth," she said.

The queen replaced the linen sample, and looking up, noticed a woman wearing a red scarf, staring at Althea, *longingly and almost jealously.* Without thinking, the queen reached for her daughter's hand, returning her gaze toward the woman—who was gone. Had she seen this woman before? Was she part of another abduction attempt? Should they leave the market every time someone stared at them?

"Althea, select a linen color you would like for your dress and the baby's bed shirt." The queen placed her hand above her eyes to block the sun's glare as she looked for the red scarf.

She felt her heart beat increase. She wanted to run to the castle, but her duty was to prepare Althea for the throne—make her strong. She placed her hand over her heart. A few seconds later one of the disguised knight's asked, "Yes, my queen?"

"There was a woman staring at Althea a minute ago. I think I have seen her before."

"What did she look like?"

"Blue eyes, sandy blonde hair, red scarf, and my height," she said.

"I'll inform the other Long Bows."

The queen's nerves relaxed. Six people were now keeping watch for the woman in the red scarf.

"Mother, I am hungry. May we have a pasty for lunch?"

"Yes my dear. The bakery is around the corner."

Stopping at the bakery, she and her daughter had a beef pasty on the bench out front. Althea finished her turnover and wiped her mouth on a handkerchief from her pocket. She swung her feet and waved in the direction of the leather goods shop. The queen looked in that direction. No one was there except the juggler.

Am I getting paranoid?

"Althea, who are you waving to?"

"A lady. Over there." She pointed in the juggler's direction. The queen saw the two disguised knights enter the small alley. A minute later, one of the knights appeared next to the bench.

"My queen, we have caught a woman wearing a green scarf."

"Green scarf?"

"Yes ma'am. She was waving to the princess. We decided to detain her. She fits the description except for the scarf."

"Where is she now?"

"We took her to the jail where it is private."

"Please, take us there."

The market's murmur quieted as the vendors and customers watched five Long Bows surrounding the queen and princess as they walked to the castle. The queen fiddled with her shirtsleeves. Couldn't they walk any faster?

Inside the safety of the castle walls, her nerves settled slightly. *Were they being watched?*

She knelt, examined the area—all was safe, and touched her daughter's arm.

"Althea dear, I have to talk with someone for a while. These two Long Bows will take you to my meeting room. You can draw with Bettina."

"What is wrong, Mother?"

"I will be up in a little while."

The queen took a deep breath to calm her nerves. She smoothed her clothes while watching Althea walk away between the two Long Bows across the brick cul-de-sac.

Before taking the first stair, Althea stopped, turned, and waved. The queen smiled and returned Althea's wave. Francine started for the jail, then stopped, and watched Althea climb the seven stairs and walk through the doors opened by the two escorts.

The doors closed.

The queen walked toward the jail. *Maybe this was the same woman we have encountered several times in the market.*

She took several deep breaths to calm her mind before she entered.

Inside the room were four rickety chairs. The interior plaster walls were mostly a dingy grey color with a few other colors where leftover paint had been used. A number of coin-sized paint chips had fallen and were collecting on the floor. A single barred window was in the same wall as the entrance. On the back wall was a single door leading to the cells. Several oil lamps were required to light the cold room.

Two Long Bows stood near the door. A blonde woman sat inside and stared at the floor. Her hair hung around her head like blinders. Her clothes were not of nobility quality, but were better than that of the farmer's work revealed by her hands. On another chair were three scarves—blue, green, and red.

"Please leave us alone," she said to the knights.

"But—" he began.

"It is no longer a request. Leave us. Wait outside the door."

Both knights exited the room and the queen closed the door. She walked to the other chair. The woman looked up to meet Francine's eyes. In the dimly lit room, the queen could see it—the thin petite nose, thin pearl pink lips, oval face, sandy blonde hair, and those vivid blue eyes.

"What is your name? Where are you from?" the queen asked.

The woman hesitated, "My queen, I cannot tell you these details without violating secrets I have sworn to keep."

The queen wanted to say, "*Do not test me, I am the queen,*" but she decided to take a different approach. "Whom do you have an oath with?"

"The king."

A feeling, like a forest fire, developed in Francine's stomach. *Could this be the moment she feared?*

"You are my daughter's natural mother?"

The woman stared at the queen, raised her eyebrows, then let out a long exhale.

"Yes, my queen," she replied.

"What is your name? Where are you from?"

"Samantha Hamilton. I live about two hours north of the castle."

"Why did you give her up?"

"We were just married and could not afford a child. My husband fell from the roof while replacing the sod. I could not care for him, the farm, and our upcoming baby."

"How did Oscar, I assume, know about your child?"

"We are neighbors of Oscar and Abbey."

The queen rose from the chair and paced the small interrogation and admitting area.

"What did my husband trade or pay for *our* daughter, and your silence?"

"Every three months, Oscar stops by with money, to help pay the mortgage, buy seed, clothes, and tools."

"For how long?"

"Until the king dies."

The queen's anger escalated as she paced. Suddenly, the impact of the scheme's required silence was clear. She stopped pacing.

"Can I go now?" Samantha wiped her sweaty palms on her cotton dress and rested her long, slender hands on her knees.

"No!" The woman looked at the queen with red, tearful eyes, and directed her eyes to the floor.

"What day was she born?" the queen asked.

"November fourth."

"Did you give birth at your house?"

"No, we were in Saraton with two Long Bows. Oscar showed up about a week before she was born. He departed for the castle the day after her birth. We left to return to our farm the next day with the two guards."

"Have you or your husband told anyone about this?"

"Just you." Their eyes met.

"We need to keep it that way. This meeting is our special secret—not even our husbands need know. Agreed?"

Samantha rubbed her fingers through her hair. Her eyes were on the floor. "Ag... ," she whispered. She continued to stare at the floor for a few moments, and then suddenly looked into the queen's eyes as if she were searching for a sign.

"Agreed," she said.

"I want you to know I love Althea. And I will do for her what I think best."

"May I meet her?" Samantha asked.

"Yes. But not right now. I will arrange a meeting, soon."

The queen opened the door. The guards, who may or may not have heard their conversation still stood outside the walls. "This is not the woman I saw," she said.

The guards nodded. "What is your wish my queen?"

"Escort this woman back to the market," Francine said. She glanced at Samantha. "I apologize for any problems we may have created for you."

* * *Bettina* * *

"Hello, Bettina."

The princess inspected Bettina's drawing.

"Hello, Althea." She clinched her teeth and her stomach muscles tightened.

"Mother is talking to some woman in the jail. May I draw with you until she arrives?" Althea had already removed her coat and hung it on the chair's back.

"Yes, here is some paper and charcoal." Bettina replied. *Why do you have so much and I have nothing?*

The two bodyguards looked to each other. "She is safe now. We may depart."

"Enjoy the rest of your day, princess."

"Thank you."

The two bodyguards left.

"What should I draw?" Althea asked.

"Some good pictures in that book of birds. Or you could draw the market."

"That is what I will draw, the market."

The king entered.

"Oh...what are you doing here?" he said.

The king's posture stiffened, his head shaking slightly as he crossed his arms.

"We are drawing, Father." Althea held up her picture of the market to show him.

"That is nice." He turned to Bettina. "And you are the archbishop's niece?"

"Yes, your majesty." Bettina stood.

"Excuse me for a moment, I need something from the queen's desk." He moved her aside.

The king reached inside the drawer and withdrew five envelopes. He noticed the smudges. An examination of his hands revealed they were covered with charcoal. He wiped his hands on his shirt, leaving black streaks. He inspected the desktop and the chair arms—they were covered with charcoal dust.

Bettina watched as the king's eyes moved between his smudged shirt, his hands, and Althea's dress. He shook his head before he held out his arms with his palms to the ceiling.

"Althea, what is that on your clothes?" he asked.

"Charcoal."

"Who brought that into the castle?" His voice grew louder.

"I did, your majesty," Bettina muttered.

"Clean up this mess! Throw out those sheets with the infernal charcoal on them. I want this all gone and this room cleaned immediately." Again, he crossed his arms.

"But sir, they are my drawings."

"*I do not care*. We cannot have everything covered in charcoal dust!" He slammed the door as he exited.

They were silent for a while.

"I guess we had better clean up," Althea said. Bettina's breathing was heavy. Her ears were even turning red.

Bettina watched the floor for several minutes. "All right," she said finally.

* * *

Bettina walked down the hall, passing the king's meeting room. He was in her head a lot. One day she would be free of his bothersome, selfish nature.

There was a loud striking sound followed by the king's voice penetrating the oaken door.

"The cathedral funding meeting is in two days. And Thomas is not getting any more money until the stable construction is complete. Our horses are more important than books and art. The cathedral is fine for now."

Bettina went to the maids' quarters. Her appetite had vanished.

She felt numb and discouraged. Her jaw was clenched ever so tightly and she'd recently made a habit of grinding her teeth.

I am now living in the maid's quarters. At home, I used to have my own room. The king's actions have made Uncle Thomas's life miserable. I have nothing left—not even my drawings. I understand now why Thomas warned me about the king. He really is trying to make our lives difficult.

She decided Uncle Thomas should know. Walking to the cathedral, each step intensified the angered hue of her crimson face.

* * Francine * *

That evening the queen locked herself in her meeting room. She refused to answer the king's inquiries through the locked door, and when she'd had enough of his breathing, Francine took it upon herself to go a step further.

When she tossed the book to the door the shadow beneath disappeared.

The single oil lamp on the desk provided little light to the dark beyond the desktop. Her mood was darker than the faint shadows on the walls.

I was deceived! She thought as she paced the floor.

She imagined the king persuading Oscar to be part of the scheme, Oscar spending months finding the right baby, and sneaking it into the castle at just the right moment.

What do I do if she demands her daughter back? This woman could bring down the monarchy and unravel the whole scheme. Am I willing to see if Oscar can take care of this? The law requires the successor to be thirteen years old, and be of direct linage to the king or queen...
Should I reveal my new knowledge to the king before this child is born?

She rubbed her belly. *If this baby dies, there will be no legal heir to the throne. I love Althea and cannot put her at risk. Perhaps I will know what to do after the baby is born...What did they do with the stillborn baby? Was it unilaterally disposed of without any discussion with me?*

Her heartbeat filled the silence of the castle.

Though the king had Oscar to talk with, she had *no one*, and it wasn't fair. Who could she talk to? The archbishop? No, the king would have her head. Althea? No, she was too young to understand. The king? Oscar?

It felt as if she were on a barren island. Her world had been reduced to three adults and two children—one, a very important child. The baby kicked.

Her stomach gurgled when the aroma from the lamb pasty, apple sauce, and fresh bread on the hot flat river rock tray was set outside her door. After a bite of the juicy pasty, her thoughts were hopeful this baby would be healthy.

She wiped her hands on the dinner cloth, picked up the quill—the blank page was urging her to write—the adoption facts as well as the deception. *This is the record of Queen Francine concerning the deception* the words flowed like water and slowly doused the fire of her anger. Writing had a therapeutic effect, with each word another drop of water. By the middle of the page, she understood the king's reasoning for the deception. Time was running out for them to conceive. But his reasoning was not strong enough to eliminate her current anguish.

Her anger towards the king remained strong. His heart may have been in the right place, but his implementation was poor. Why hadn't the king consulted her? How would she have responded to this charade? Were there other schemes?

Her irritation directed earlier at Oscar waned for he was the king's servant. Once the king had presented his scheme, Oscar had had to execute its directives. A scheme with this level of deception required limiting the participants—she reasoned some might even have been removed as the scheme progressed. Had he done this to protect his family?

Tears dripped slowly onto the paper as she reviewed it; in time the bottom edge became soggy and wet, but the letter had to be written and completed. Her peace of mind wouldn't return for several days. Until then she would blame the weird urges of pregnancy for her recent behavior. She hoped the king would accept her answer.

Sleeping on the floor in her meeting room was uncomfortable. But like the sun clearing the morning fog, her mind was clear and she had a plan. Of course she could burn the letter, but she wanted a last word with the king regarding his lack of trust.

With renewed determination, she placed the sealed letter addressed to Althea in her Bible on the top shelf.

Like quicksand, she was too deep in the king's scheme to speak up now, and being still was safer than a lot of thrashing about.

* * *Louis* * *

The chapel, built first, had later been attached to the castle now constructed around it. Several layers of lacquer sealed the silver and gold painted walls. A large cubed rock functioned as the altar. Two pottery vases on the altar carried seasonal flowers—a collage of colorful daisies. Four benches on either side of the room faced the altar at an angle.

The king's first trip to the chapel left him unsure of what to do. He sat on the front bench near the wall, then moved to the center of the chapel, and finally sat on the second row to use the kneeling pad. Pressing his palms together felt awkward. Interlacing his fingers seemed uncomfortable. Leaning on his elbows with his hands on his cheeks felt natural.

"Hello, I have had five stillborn boys," he prayed to no one in particular. "Their deaths have been hard to accept. We, Francine and I, would like an heir to the throne. We are getting older. I am not a religious man, more superstitious. If a curse has been cast on me, please spare Francine from my predicament and help her deliver a healthy baby. Amen."

He stood from his kneeling position and took a seat on the front bench, and wondered again about the queen. She had not been happy since she'd thrown the book.

* * *

Oscar entered the chapel, the dust from the ride still on his clothes. He quietly sat on the backbench before the king noticed him.

"How was your mission?"

"Unsuccessful, I am sorry to report."

"We were lucky with Althea."

"How is Althea?" Oscar asked. "I haven't seen her since the birthday party."

"She is doing fine," the king replied. "I was concerned she might get jealous, but she seems excited for a sister or brother. Bettina is keeping her busy. The assistant cook gave Bettina some new dustless drawing stick."

"Hunter, the assistant cook?"

"Yes. Why do you ask?"

"Just curious. I will discuss my thoughts with you when I have more information."

Fifth Son

Originally, the queen's smaller bedroom had been designed for a royal child, but she was happy because it was big enough for her bed, dresser, vanity, two chairs, and night stands. Four oil lamps provided the light, two at the vanity, one on the wall, and one on the nightstand. When the room was used for births, two chambermaids waited outside with fresh water buckets. A doorway on the opposite wall from the entry accessed the anteroom and a hallway to all the royal family bedrooms.

Smiling, in spite of the exertion and sweat that poured from her body, the queen pushed. Exhausted after five hours of labor, she found the will from deep within to continue. She pushed on cramped muscles, fought through momentary blackouts, bit so hard her jaw line ached; even individual teeth pulsated from the gnashing. The final, satisfying push gave birth to a baby. She waited what seemed a long time before the baby cried, but it was a wonderful sound.

As she received the baby, the queen noticed the midwife's pleasant smile.

The queen lifted the baby—*good weight.* She pulled back the edge of the blanket—*good color.* The queen whispered, "You are so precious. I think you are going to make it." *Finally, after five deaths we have two healthy children.* Caught inspecting the baby, a guilty grin momentarily graced her face before she returned her gaze to the healthy pink baby. *Finally we have a baby of our own—after seven struggling years. In a peculiar way we have a family—Bettina the orphan, Althea the adopted princess, and this baby—the Prince.*

I am a mother!

As their eyes met the king's rare smile brought her great satisfaction. The king opened the door and told one of the maids to get Althea.

He closed the door.

"He's beautiful. How do you like the name Quentin? It means 'fifth son'," the king asked. He touched the baby's tiny hands and feet.

The queen knew Quentin was really their sixth child, but she would discuss that with the king later.

"It is fitting," she said.

"Can I hold him?"

The midwife quickly glanced at Francine who handed Quentin to Louis.

As the king spoke baby talk, the midwife and maids giggled.

Althea, wearing the yellow linen dress the royal seamstress had made, smiled when she saw the baby.

The king sat so that Althea could see the baby.

"Althea, you have a new brother," the queen said.

"He is so tiny," Althea said. A faint whistle as the baby exhaled made her snicker. "He already snores. Can I touch him?"

"Yes, but be gentle," the king replied.

She touched the small palm, and Quentin's hand gripped her finger.

"What's his name? What's this red spot on his ear?" Quentin stretched and his peaceful yawn filled the room. Francine watched as a contented expression appeared on the maids' faces.

"His name is Quentin. The red spot is a birthmark," the queen said.

"Hello, Quentin. I'm your sister, Althea."

"We should put him in the bassinette so he can rest," the midwife said.

"Let me hold him a little while before I nap," the queen said when she heard the gurgling.

The king handed Quentin to the queen, and then kissed her forehead.

She noticed the pause and caught his eyes looking away before he rose.

* * *Althea* * *

Two days passed, and the color of her Mother's face was still red. Althea wondered why Mother slept so much.

"Is this normal?" she heard her father ask the midwife, "Have you handled this type of problem before?" He touched the queen's forehead. "She seems feverish."

Althea held Mother's hand hoping that if she concentrated enough a portion of her spirit and youth would make Mother well.

"This is the first time for me. Not to worry. She is probably exhausted and needs her rest." The midwife ordered everyone from the room. "My king, I will stay with her tonight."

Althea ignored the order—a princess has privileges. She glanced at Father for confirmation, who nodded toward the door as he whispered, "You need your sleep."

Althea arrived early the next morning. Mother's chin was trembling and her color had faded to match the color of the cow's milk.

The king wiped the queen's head with a damp rag. "How do you think she is doing?" he asked the midwife.

"Her temperature increased through most of the night, causing her to sweat. I changed her bedding twice. When her temperature reached its highest point, her neck twitched along with the mumbling and shivering."

The king reached for her mother's hand.

Mother's whole body began shivering like being in a snowstorm without a coat. Suddenly, Mother gasped for air, then her breathing returned to normal.

Althea was sure Mother's illness was her fault. Mother had never been sick and she couldn't remember a day without her. Althea restrained her crying, because Father had emphasized the need to be emotionally stronger than a man to be respected as queen.

"Francine, keep fighting. I need you. Quentin and Althea need you," Father petitioned as he wiped her mother's forehead.

The sickness continued until the third day. Father said her mother had a normal temperature, and her pink color provided hope. But by late afternoon the high temperature had returned and then came the terrible words.

"*Do not take her!*" The words came from her mother, lying still on the bed.

Althea jumped. Her mother was not awake. Her father felt her forehead.

Althea saw her father's eyes widen and he momentarily lifted his hand from Mother's forehead.

"The fever is returning," he said. A few seconds later his head dropped.

"Leave the room, but please wait outside," the king said.

"Samantha, where did you come from?" the queen muttered in her sleep.

"Shhh," he whispered, trying to quiet her.

The queen's arms flailed, striking her father twice. Just as quickly the movement stopped. He placed her arms back under the blankets.

"Is Mother all right?" Althea asked. A strange feeling came over her. She knew something was wrong, but did not know what.

"*I am deceived,*" the queen said.

Father held Mother's hand and stared at her face for a long time. Her eyes opened. The queen's soft voice whispered something. She took a couple of deep breaths, closed her eyes briefly, and repeated the words, "I am deceived."

Althea could no longer hold back the tears as she watched. Father held mother's hand—she no longer held his. When his head rested on her shoulder, Althea knew her mother was gone.

* * *

Father roamed the dark hallways by night, slept in the morning, and drank in the afternoon and evening. *A smelly ogre with a terrible cough must have replaced his soul because he was unusually mean to the castle staff. He talked to the queen. That awful cough was loud. The more he drank, the more time he spent with his head in a bucket—he did not even eat.*

On the fourth afternoon of the queen's death, Althea went into the queen's bedroom. She sat in the corner on the floor behind the chest of drawers and stared at the empty bed. Althea wished her mother would walk through the door. After almost an hour of alternating between the bed and the door, she crossed her arms on her knees, and rested her head.

"Goodbye Mother," she whispered.

In that moment she heard footsteps. The door latch rubbed the door. The slow motion of the door extended the awful squeaking hinges. Her heart was anxious. No one entered. Maybe it was Mother's ghost.

Father walked in and closed the door. Althea watched him. He gently ran his hand along the length of the bed and pulled the bedspread back opening a triangle that exposed the pillow. His flat hand moved slowly across it. He lifted the pillow to his face and took a deep breath. In a few moments, he was asleep on the queen's bed, mumbling something that Althea couldn't understand.

She silently left the room.

Nanny Takes Over

Oscar worried about the messages the king had sent Althea and the castle staff with his drunken suffering. He searched the stables, barracks, the king's bedroom and meeting room, the assembly hall, and the dining room. His pace quickened as he searched. *He hoped to find him before he made a spectacle of himself.*

He found the king in the queen's bedroom.

"King Louis, wake up, wake up!" Oscar waited a minute, but there was no response. "*Louis! Wake-up!*" He shook the king's shoulders.

Twice Louis wiped his dry teeth with his tongue.

"Where am I?" the king asked. A few moments later Louis lifted his head slightly, opened his eyes long enough to look around, and then confidently nodded once.

He moaned as his aching joints resisted movement. His eyes were once again closed as both hands gently massaged his temples. "Oh my, this is the worst headache."

Oscar took a deep breath and rolled his eyes.

"My king, it is not fair to you. But you must let her go and mourn in private. You need to be strong for Manshire Province, and those who are still alive."

"I need to focus on relieving this suffering," the king said.

Oscar covered his nose as he approached the king. "A warm bath is what you need first."

King Louis III sat upright on the edge of Francine's bed.

"Understood." Oscar observed the slight lifting of the stone face, the exaggerated eye roll until their eyes met. The king's sense of humor was not yet awake.

"Oscar, I miss Francine. Have you looked at Quentin? He is a tiny Francine—small face, perky nose, long neck, petite hands, and those large brown eyes that see into my soul." He rubbed his temples for a few seconds then continued, "Bring Bettina here. And Oscar, thank you for your concern."

Searching for Bettina, Oscar wondered why the king wanted to see her. The king was bathing when Oscar escorted Bettina to the king's bedroom. In the mirror, Oscar noticed Bettina's surprise at the unmade bed and clothes laying on the floor, chair, dresser, and writing desk. Oscar picked up the clothes on the path to the bathroom door.

Bettina knocked.

"Who goes there?" The sound was muffled, but still clear.

"Bettina, my king."

"Quentin is going to need fulltime care. Are you available for the job? The queen thinks...thought highly of you," he said.

Oscar closed his eyes and shook his head in doubt. Did he just hear the king ask the help of his archenemy's niece?

"I would be honored to serve the king."

The words placed an invisible dagger within his heart. Something was not right. Even her voice sounded...she seemed too eager, or maybe just happy to have a job?

* * *Bettina* * *

Bettina checked on Quentin. Satisfied the nap would last a while, she ran across the street to the cathedral. She rubbed the medallion's engraved ship to calm her nerves. It was partially rubbed away, but it didn't matter.

She heard the thick dark curtain in the adjacent compartment being pulled across the hand carved walnut grill. "What is it my child?" the archbishop asked.

"Uncle Thomas, I am the caretaker for the king's son, Quentin," she whispered.

Except for the drumming of fingers in the adjacent compartment there was silence. "Excellent. Your must care for this child as though he were your own. We have waited a long time for this opportunity. This perfectly fits into my plan. Meet me tomorrow after sunset at the marsh west of Camel Humps."

* * *

Bettina made her way in the dark. A quarter moon shown between the drifting clouds illuminating the smooth surface of the rocks. A chilly north wind made her wish she had gloves and a scarf.

A torch would have attracted attention from the rear guard.

Out of sight from the guard tower she approached the dim torchlight from deep inside the forested area surrounding the marsh. The pungent scent of the stale marsh water irritated her nose, but she did not sneeze, though she fell more than once. Her hands were scuffed on the rough stepping stones, or the mushy forest floor squished its acrid smelly mud between her fingers

At Camel Humps, she entered the torch lit hideout rubbing her bleeding hands.

"What happened?"

"I fell. Twice."

"Let me look at them." The archbishop offered his monogrammed handkerchief as a bandage. "Be careful. The king cannot see your hands in this condition. It might pique his interest and the questioning could expose my plan."

"Understood."

"We will hold these meetings in the dawn hour when the rest of the kingdom is asleep. I will lower the red sash on the cathedral tower window to signal our meetings. Bettina, are you prepared to take the time needed to achieve our full vengeance?"

"Yes."

"Here is my plan. For the first five years we will raise him as the king's son."

Bettina flipped her coat's collar up and closed the neckline.

"From age five to nine, we will slowly build up his ego and dreams of being the king. At age ten, we will need to control most of the communication by keeping the monarchy from talking with Quentin. To occupy the king, I will create some diversions. You will need to create excuses to keep the king from his son, and the sister from her brother. But, for now, we need to establish you as Quentin's trusted guardian."

She was excited that life had finally blessed her with the opportunity to avenge her parents' death and the menial life forced upon her. But she was unhappy with uncle Thomas's time frame. She remembered stories about eight year old kings.

* * *Oscar* * *

Oscar delivered his horse to the stables to have it brushed and fed. A quick survey would permit him to answer the king's questions at the stable construction meeting. He encountered the king coming down from the residents' floor.

"Getting a late start today?" Oscar asked. He knew what was coming next.

"I have been watching Bettina through the open door," answered the king. "She changed Quentin's diaper and hummed a lullaby. Quentin's giggle was wonderful—it filled the room, the adjacent hallway, and my heart. It was enjoyable until I saw Quentin's face. He looks so much like Francine. I wish I could get beyond my pain, but these twenty-four months after her passing, I still deeply miss her."

Oscar had run out of fresh responses. "It is unfortunate you are unable to spend more time with him,"

"Yes, and considering the trouble we had with stillborn babies, we are lucky to have children," the king said. "Too many babies are dying at birth. I have missed a lot of sleep wondering if I had brought this curse on the kingdom. Could nature be punishing me for the scheme to substitute Althea at birth? Could it be for going to war with Saraton? Or, was it because I deceived Francine?"

"You have dealt with pressure and controversy before," Oscar replied. "But, this time you should consider a talk with the archbishop."

* * *Louis* * *

The office's new desk was much larger and came with a platform four inches above the floor. The king now looked down on anyone seated in the two chairs. An oil lamp, one on each corner opposite the king's chair, partially blocked the visitor's view.

"Archbishop Thomas, have a seat."

"Thank you." Thomas moved the chair.

"Our relationship has been rocky, at best, but I would like to call a truce to get your thoughts on the baby deaths."

The archbishop leaned forward in the chair. "I have given this much thought as well, and my conclusions are these: a curse, a new disease, or something in the water."

"Curse? Do curses last longer than a few months?" The king felt his four sons had been the victims of a curse.

"Yes, some can last a lifetime."

"Can we un-curse?"

"Like an exorcism?"

"Yes." The king had easily directed the conversation to this point, but it was the same face he saw now as before, Thomas on the raft—twisted, confused, and angry.

"Is that what you think I do—ward off evil spirits?" The archbishop folded his arms and pressed his back against the chair.

Louis held out his hands with his palms open to Thomas.

"Relax, Thomas. I am looking for a solution. And you are the most educated man in the area." He inhaled, paused a moment, exhaled, and placed his hands on the chair arms.

"I have heard the number of deaths are declining," King Louis III said.

"Yes, but I think less people are getting pregnant," Archbishop Thomas, replied. "Fewer couples are asking for the Blessing of the Womb."

"It's been three years. Could this be the new definition of normal?" he asked opening his hands with the palms facing each other.

The archbishop drummed his fingers on the chair's arms. His eyes were closed for a few seconds then came the stone faced stare. He raised the index finger of his left hand and pointed at the ceiling.

"I feel there is a disease that will run its course. Or, the curse will be lifted. Or, maybe it *really* is something in the water." He paused.

Louis knew Thomas held something back as the archbishop began to search for words. "This will pass...and we will never...really know the...source. I do feel the end is close."

The king's thoughts were similar and there was something beyond his understanding about this problem. "I hope you are right. I am so happy Quentin was born before this started."

"Yes, that is fortunate," the archbishop said. His gaze went to somewhere above the king's head, and his jaw clenched.

"Thank you for sharing your thoughts with me. By the way, Bettina is wonderful with Quentin. Her reports on his progress are quite satisfying."

"Yes, the queen has done a wonderful job of improving her outlook on life," the archbishop said, "though we had to stop her drawings because that infernal charcoal was getting on and into everything."

The archbishop glared at Louis for a moment then lowered his eyes to the floor.

"Are we done?" Thomas asked.

"Yes."

The archbishop rose, picked up his hat, and walked out. His fingers drummed the hat's brim until he placed it on his head as he reached for the door handle.

ANDEAN WHITE

Righting the Ships

* * Thomas * *

The librarian's knock rattled the thick oak door to his chambers—"Enter."

"Your grace, this letter came in the church's postal pouch."

"Thank you."

It was from the office of the Smythe Family Shipping Company.

Thomas Smythe:

I regret to inform you that your sister Regina has died, and you are the next in line for ownership according to our bylaws. Please inform us of your desires. We will continue to operate the company as before until we hear from you.

Sincerely,

William Whitman
Operations Manager
Smythe Family Shipping Company

Regina, Thomas's older sister, had been the head of the family business, as Father had been busy being the minister of monetary issues. Her head for numbers had made her the perfect replacement for Father. For this reason, Thomas only shed a few tears—he and Regina had not been that close. The only connection he remembered was in his youth. She'd come to him every afternoon to study and practice music.

When Thomas announced his pursuit of an archbishop career—Father had withdrawn his offer to take over as president. The next day Father had named Regina the future president of Smythe Family Freight Company.

Regina didn't have a family. She was smart and rich, but not very pretty. Her fiancé enjoyed music and art, but left when he perceived her job was a higher priority than he was.

The bottom line: Thomas and Bettina were the last two living Smythes. A relationship that even Thomas thought was taxing.

Thomas left his chambers. He informed the priest he would be gone for a few months while he took care of the family business, and placed him in charge.

Yes, there was something else to do. Thomas shivered at the thought.

It was a short walk and a longer pause outside the queen's door to see Bettina, but at last he called out, "Bettina."

"Uncle Thomas?"

"Yes."

"Come in. Please."

The girl had several drawings laid out on the floor— birds, landscapes, people, and the castle. He was awestruck. Her skill was strong.

A particular drawing caught his attention. Dressed in a white full-length skirt and shirt with a gold cupa draped over its shoulders, hovered a translucent angel. The halo formed the base of the priest's pointed hat. Archbishop Thomas saw himself as the angel overlooking the king's grave.

The spine of a personal journal rested on the left side of the desk under the window. Steam from a cup of tea blurred the opposite corner of the window's frame. Through the window, a white cross rose out of a fresh mound of dirt.

"These are beautiful," he said, though a burning anger towards the king filled his throat.

"I only have time as Quentin naps. Althea lets me use the meeting room as long as I keep it charcoal free. Hunter, the assistant cook, gave me this stylus from his home country of Saraton. It does not leave charcoal dust and it stays sharper longer."

"This is wonderful! Does the king know?" he asked.

"If he does, he is not complaining, or he is conceding because I am taking care of Quentin."

He reviewed the drawings for a few minutes. *Her skill was really quite wonderful.*

"I came by to tell you your aunt Regina has died."

There was a period of silence, but nothing more.

"I did not know her very well," the girl said finally. "We visited her just a few times at the docks and enjoyed all that hectic activity. Mother said Aunt Regina was too smart to talk to."

"You and I are the last of the Smythe family," Uncle Thomas said. The statement stirred thoughts of his mother and sister Rebecca, Bettina's mother. Surprisingly, he felt closer to Bettina.

"I am taking a leave to deal with the shipping company," he continued. "I should be back in less than three months. The librarian and priest know how to find me. Are you going to be fine while I'm gone?"

"I will be fine, Uncle Thomas." He heard the confidence in her voice and saw it in her eyes.

Maybe it was the reality that he and Bettina were the last of the Smythe family, or that he had finally won the argument with his father. Regardless, he felt a little melancholy.

"Bettina, you have turned into a wonderful young lady." Thomas kissed her forehead. "After we execute my revenge plans, you should consider an art career."

"I can be good when I need to be," she answered rather flatly.

* * *

Manshire Port was surrounded by small hills that sheltered it from the wind, and the long narrow channel protected it from ocean storms. In the summer, white sheep grazed on the slopes. Its capacity was fifteen ships; there were eight unoccupied docks. Half a mile away, the view from the crest of the road reminded Thomas of ants preparing for winter. Crates were off-loaded from a ship to another or to the holding warehouse until it was placed on another ship or delivered in Manshire. On the far side of the inlet were the yellow offices of the Smythe Family Shipping Company. Two of their four docks were empty.

On the near side was the competitor—Seafarer Shipping. At the east end of the bay was the empty blue warehouse and office of Rochester and Son—the donator of the three small casks of silver coins that had been conveniently left out of Father's medallion story.

Thomas missed the thick and salty sea air. As he approached the end of the road, he faintly heard the dockworkers. He never understood how simultaneously workers could be yelling at different people and still have the right activities happen.

Four hundred yards from the office, Thomas hobbled his horse and locked the wagon brake. Access to the office was by dock, the same dock bustling with crates, dollies, wagons, and dockworkers—strong, burly men who would cut your throat for grog money. He had walked this dock many times as a boy, but never in archbishop's clothing. As he walked across the docks, an eerie silence surrounded him. Dockworkers moved aside to clear a path. A feeling of power satisfied his ego.

William met him at the door.

"Welcome Thomas, or should I say Archbishop Thomas?"

"Thomas is fine."

"How was your trip?"

"I am happy it is only a three hour ride. Show me around so I can get my sea legs." Thomas wanted William uncomfortable and thought getting right to business was the answer.

The full tour took about an hour. William spent time showing off their new efficient weighing scales, how the paperwork was handled, and the fine warehouse expansion. His eagerness and presentation revealed his desire to keep his job.

The warehouse was a beehive of activity, workers going in and out with crates on squeaky wheeled carts, like birds chirping. Ironically, that sound had driven the birds from the warehouse. Loose floor planks slapped the framework as the wheels crossed over them. The air, cooled by the ocean breeze, drifted through the open doors on both ends of the warehouse, and the smell of the water eight feet below the flooring brought back memories of the last time he'd visited here. Still, this was where Father had first said, *"What kind of job is archbishop? I cannot respect your job choice. Who will run this company after I retire?"*

"William, can I stay in the warehouse?" he asked suddenly. Thomas hoped this deepened William's discomfort.

William hesitated. "It is your warehouse."

"What is the best way to move my things in?"

"There is a new road around the cove. I will have one of the men drive your wagon around."

"Plan to review the books tomorrow. Where can I get a meal?"

"I would be happy to bring a meal to you."
"That is very thoughtful."

* * *

William arrived early to gather the books for the review, but Thomas was already reviewing the log entries.

As the operations manager hired by Father, and endorsed by Regina, his decisions were always in the best interest of the family business, or so the archbishop had always been told. In his early fifties, he would be retiring soon, and for job security a backup had not been trained. His hair had gone silver in his late thirties and working in the sun had leathered his face, making him look a decade older than his actual age. The man enjoyed material objects like having the best wagon, the most groomed horse, the most elegant house, and the best clothes money could buy. He appeared to care for the business, as if it was his own.

Initially, the books appeared to be in good condition; then Thomas noticed that the bank balance was slowly dwindling. Previously, with Regina it had increased one to two percent a year, but now the balance forward in the bank ledger was a hundred less at the top of each new page—eight pages since Regina's last entry. At the current rate of embezzling, in twenty-seven months the account balance would be zero.

"I need a couple weeks to digest all this information and observe the operation," Thomas said. He had already made up his mind, but he would watch the business to validate his decision.

"If I can get you more information, please do not hesitate to ask," William replied.

"I have what I need at this time." Thomas could see the bulge of William's medallion under his shirt. He was the only person outside the family to wear one. It reminded him of the other version of the medallion story.

Smythe's family shipping business was about to declare bankruptcy. William, a heavy drinker in those days, suggested they bribe the port master to direct some business their way—like the other shipping companies. He suggested they "borrow" three casks of silver coins from a competitor's pallet. William could dump the coins in a crate and put the empty casks back on the pallet. Within four months the blue warehouse of Rochester and Son went out of business. It was a year following the business failure that Gilford Rochester died from pneumonia. At the funeral, several referred to him by his nickname Skunk—one being his son Howard, also known as Skunk Junior.

Archbishop Thomas stopped at the recently painted port church to visit with the vicar. Thomas had served here as the vicar before his transfer. Blue trim on the roofline, stained glass windows, and doorframes of the bright white church had recently been repainted. Flowerbeds were tilled waiting for spring, and the white fence needed a few pickets replaced.

"Welcome Archbishop Thomas, it has been some time."

"Yes Vicar Ernest. It is good to see you."

Thomas looked around and was impressed by the cleanliness of the floors and benches. He was jealous of the support it appeared the vicar was receiving from the local authorities.

"I see the window of Samson has been restored. It is a favorite of mine."

"Yes, we had to hire a craftsmen from Manshire for the repair." They looked at the window until Vicar Earnest broke the awkward silence. "Sorry to hear about your family and Regina."

"Thank you. It was difficult to have the sudden loss of family." He waited a few moments to give the impression he was praying for them, then continued, "As the vicar here, I remember parishioners divulging significant information to me outside the confessional."

The vicar hesitated. "What are you looking for?" he asked.

"Is there someone in the area with enough money to buy a shipping company?"

"You're planning to sell?"

"Uncertain. Just checking the options," he lied, drumming his fingers at the end of the bench.

* * *

Thomas spent two weeks observing the operation. He watched warehousemen hauling crates, tying down loads, and transporting goods. It was a flurry of activity—reminded him of the market at Manshire Castle. Men were yelling across the water and docks asking for help with heavy loads, providing information to the clerks, which were recorded in the logbooks.

Until this visit, Thomas had forgotten the chaotic nature of the docks. *Another reason he'd chosen the church—no responsibility to other men whom he was afraid of.*

Each afternoon he disappeared for about two hours. Though he told others he was constantly in need of a nap, the truth was there were things he needed to do without the prying eyes of William—or someone William might trust.

To Thomas, William seemed uneasy. William was a man seeking control in every part of his life, which made him very good at his job, but made him nervous if the control fell to someone else.

On the fifteenth day Thomas left the warehouse early in the morning and returned late afternoon. At the end of the shift, he announced he had sold the business to Seafarer Shipping. He posted the list of employees that Seafarer was keeping. His confessional experience proved to be valuable, as he consoled those not hired.

Now finally, Thomas had the last word in he and his father's long-standing argument. His father's dream of being the biggest shipping company, run by his only son, was gone. He would no longer be haunted by his father's objection to his choice of jobs. He suspected Father's distaste was a fear Thomas's archbishop oath would force him to expose the medallion lie.

Thomas had no ability to control the operation from the Manshire Cathedral. The books had revealed that William could not be trusted.

William's reaction was disturbing, but not surprising. He was leaving him with nothing after all. As the man stood with his hands clamped to the edge of his former desk, glaring at Thomas seated in his former chair, it was all Thomas could do not to smile.

"*I have given my very soul to this family*," William said. "Regina recognized my value and promised me a raise, but then she died unexpectedly." A brief partial smile graced his face before his angry demeanor returned.

"Seafarer does not need another operations manager," Thomas said.

William left the desk to pace. "What am I going to do?"

"Seafarer says it would hire you as a dock worker."

William's face changed to red.

"How would you like it, if after twenty years the diocese fired you, then offered you a job as vicar?"

"I do not have to worry about that. You created this problem when you started taking company funds."

Thomas rose from the chair, walked to the door, and held it open for William to leave. The squeaky hinges covered-up William's mumbling.

All was arranged for Bettina to receive twenty-five percent of the sell price; he the other seventy-five percent. Any money left after his death would be given to Bettina. He was actually excited to tell Bettina about her inheritance.

Now, he finally had the funds to hire the help he needed.

Untidy Things

Althea realized she was walking fast and had to be mindful of others perceptions. She went down to the maids' quarters. It was a large room with two rows of twelve single beds separated by a trunk at each bed. Unlike the uniform look of the Long Bow's barracks, each bed had a unique, handmade bedspread. At the end of the room was the bathing area, which gave the room a musty smell. All the maids were out working and the room was empty. Althea gathered a coat, gloves, and a scarf. As she reached for the door, it opened, hitting her hand.

"Ouch!"

"Princess, my apologizes, I did not know you were there."

"I am all right. It was my fault for being in such a hurry." Althea looked down at the clothes draped over her arm. Her pulse quickened. "Are any of these yours?"

"No ma'am."

"I found them in the main hallway, and thought I would see if they belonged to anyone here. I will come back later this evening."

"Yes princess. Have a nice day."

Walking back to her room she decided if she had to undress from her market disguise to her regular clothing, she might be late for dinner, which would invite Father's questioning.

Althea closed the door and took a deep breath. She found an old, frayed dress that had not been worn for a while. Manually, she cut a few seams. A trip to the stables and back by the back stairwell would produce the final look she needed. Holding the top she let the dress drag behind her down the three floors of stairs. At the bottom, she bunched the hem together and let the top drag across the stairs while she returned to her room. Fresh dirt was rubbed into the fabric.

She placed the *aged* dress over hers.

Perfect!

Back down the stairs to the stables, she unlocked the door, put the coat on and buttoned it closed. She ruffled her hair and covered it with the scarf, placed the gloves in the coat pockets and peeked out the door. The twenty steps out the stable's door seemed to take forever, and tripping over the skirt hems didn't help.

She was conflicted, as fear of being caught and a sense of satisfaction for having escaped the castle, fought within her mind. Years ago, as a child, she'd been abducted from the market, but for years since she'd managed to return to the place that had also brought her the greatest joy.

She moved with the alertness of a cat stalking a mouse. Althea watched the crowd for anyone watching her. Her nerves were on edge—every bump made her flinch under the heavy coat. Even in the cool autumn air she was sweating under all the layers of clothing.

It took half an hour to calm her nerves. She finally felt safe moving within the crowd. No one expected the princess to go to market.

She pretended to shop. Touching linen reminded her of the day Mother had taught her about materials. She watched the juggler and listened to the minstrels. A sample of fresh bread and apple jam made her wish she had money to purchase. She enjoyed the freedom and escape from the castle. Satisfied by her adventure and running out of time, she returned to the stables.

Entering the castle through the stables had taken more time than expected. The partially dried sweat at her back flowed again while she waited for the stable hands to brush the horse in the nearest stall.

Althea looked both ways. Suddenly she saw Oscar walking his horse toward the stables. Her heart thumped rapidly and her hands were shaking. She backed away and hid behind some barrels.

Oscar's horse stopped near her location. Another horse was coming from the stables. It too stopped.

Althea was certain she was about to be caught.

Suddenly she heard voices.

"Sergeant, tomorrow we will meet to discuss the men's skills, and shuffle assignments to keep them alert. A couple of the young men have shown an improvement in their weaponry skills and an awareness of their protection obligations."

"Yes, sir. We should assign a couple of bodyguards to Althea. What time?"

"Mid-morning."

"See you then."

Althea felt a tingling sensation spread throughout her body; still, she needed to continue her clandestine market trips.

Althea could hear the horses moving on the brick street. Their steady rhythmic clomping slowly eased her nerves. After a short time, she ran across the alley to the stable door. She opened the door, locked it, and tiptoed up the stairs to her bedroom. She removed the borrowed coat and scarf, hid her dirtied dress, fixed her hair, and fanned her dress dry.

ANDEAN WHITE

Winter's Thief

Part Two

ANDEAN WHITE

Season of Firsts

Bettina worried last night's argument with Quentin would influence her periodic report to the king.

"Can we take a break from studying?" Quentin asked.

"We are near the end of the Homer book. We can finish in another half hour, then move on to mythology in two days."

He pushed his chair out from the table.

She reached across the table and held his wrist. "Where are you going?" she asked.

"Anywhere I do not have to study," he replied.

"It is just another half an hour."

"It will have to wait. I am the future king and I have had enough."

He jerked his arm from her grip and ran out the door.

* * *

She entered the confessional, rubbed her medallion, and waited for the heavy curtain to be drawn.

"Yes, my child," Archbishop Thomas said.

"I need your help preparing my report on Quentin," Bettina said.

"This is a first. What has happened?"

"Quentin and I had an argument last night. I do not want it to influence my report."

"Good thinking. Meet me in an hour at my chambers."

"Uncle Thomas"—she wanted to thank him, but the curtain rings were suddenly sliding across the rod.

She walked back to the library.

Bettina spent part of the hour organizing her books and study sheets left in the library last night as she'd searched for Quentin. The remaining time was used to prepare for the meeting with her uncle. She walked to her uncle's chambers, opened the door without knocking, and ignored his stare.

"My meeting is in an hour. We need to get started," Bettina said.

"The king will use any sign of weakness as an opportunity to challenge what you are saying. I think this is a result of his job—a lot of people lie to him," the archbishop said.

Bettina nodded. *I hope the rest of this meeting is more informative.*

"Heard that Quentin had an argument with you," the archbishop offered.

"I was pressing him. He was tired, I was tired and should have stopped class."

"Are there other issues that might be hindering his education?"

"I think he is frustrated. He knows something is not right, and he may be over reacting."

"Is this becoming a common reaction or an odd circumstance?" Archbishop Thomas folded his arms. "You know the king. He usually expects to find a solution or express great insight."

"So far, this behavior has been a single event," Bettina replied.

The archbishop nodded. "I think your presentation of the event is good," he said almost to himself. "You should not have any problems with your meeting." He drummed his fingers on the desktop. "Please remind me of where we are with Quentin."

"Last year the king approved educating Quentin at the cathedral library with its better books. For the first, and so far, only time, he thanked me for my dedication to Quentin for seven years. And, he specifically mentioned the preparation with color exercises, learning the alphabet, basic reading, and arithmetic tables."

* * *

Althea knocked. "Come in," the king said.

She entered the king's meeting room, hoping her shaking hands and pounding heart would not prompt the king's curiosity.

"I am afraid I have nothing new to report. Quentin continues to be a slow student. I have to present information several times before he can apply the new ideas or skills," Bettina said, remembering the many times she'd told the king about his son's awkwardness with learning.

Today he replied: "Is there anything I can do to help him?"

"I am not sure. May I ask my Uncle Thomas? Aunt Regina once tutored uncle Thomas at home. Maybe he has some suggestions."

"Yes, yes. Give that a try," the king replied.

Bettina was surprised by his speedy approval. The time she'd practiced with the archbishop simulating the king's reactions had been wasted, and Bettina felt cheated.

* * *

"Uncle Thomas, we are making progress. It is slow, but, it is progress. The king believes Quentin is unfit to be king at 'his current level of learning'. He thinks you and I are developing an alternative plan to improve his mind."

"Excellent. In a year you will tell the king it did not work. We can continue to influence Quentin's thinking to our benefit. By the way, how is he really doing?" the archbishop asked.

"He is actually quite smart and quick to draw valid conclusions on new knowledge. His intuition is good. You will need to provide him with sound reasoning to keep him under your control as he gets older."

"You look troubled."

"This is just taking too long. Can we exact our revenge now?"

"Patience. The final blow will be worth the wait. We have had a long list of events with the king. He has caused you and I great pain, loss, and suffering. I want to be sure his suffering is equal to ours. The rumor he may resign his position for poor health is being repeated frequently. And seeing his daughter's assassination will bring him great pain. Then after his son takes control he will have great satisfaction—until he realizes we control Quentin. By law, Quentin cannot take the throne until he is thirteen. It's only six more years."

"Can we keep Quentin from the king for another six years?"

"Perhaps it's time to remind the prince that the king will never be able to separate his son's life from his wife's death."

* * *Thomas* * *

The long lines of the support columns blended into the pointed arches—stirring the archbishop's thoughts to Heaven if only for a moment. The stained glass depictions of Christ's life included two matched windows of Easter. Extra candles illuminated the paintings of Moses, Abraham, Samson, Noah, Paul and other men from the

Bible. During past sermons, he'd watched several people looking at the ceiling paintings, but not today.

Looking into the parishioner's faces, he saw their interest. One particular face captured his attention—a female with twin girls on her right and a man's arm, probably her husband's, around her on the left.

Fussy children squirmed on the pews, and an increase of baby crying signaled time to end the sermon.

He returned to his cathedra, drummed his fingers on the arm momentarily, and whispered to the priest, who'd then left the podium. A minute later the priest was talking to the ushers in the rear of the auditorium.

After the closing prayer, the archbishop watched ushers direct people to exit doors. A husband, wife, and twins were separated from their line and staged to meet the archbishop.

The archbishop saw her about fifteen people back standing in front of her bored and anxious husband who appeared to be counting the people in front of him.

Thomas had to be careful—he caught himself staring at the woman.

The archbishop knelt and greeted the first twin. "Welcome, I am Archbishop Thomas."

The twin turned to her mother.

"Go ahead. It's all right," the mother said.

"I am Elsa."

"Nice to meet you." He turned his attention to the other twin. "And you are?"

"I am Erma."

He placed a hand on the outside shoulder of each twin.

"Welcome to the cathedral. Your dresses are very nice."

"Thank you," they said in unison.

He introduced himself. "Archbishop Thomas."

"Samantha."

"Have we met before?"

"Not that I can recall. This is our first service. We waited for the girls to grow up."

"You must be the father. You have a very nice family. Your girls are very pretty."

"Yes sir. Thank you. I'm Reginald Hamilton."

"Did you have a long ride this morning?"

"Not bad. A little less than two hours."

"Where are you from?"

"The north."

"We hope to see you again," he said. He turned his attention to Samantha and looked into her crystal blue eyes. "It was nice to meet you."

* * *Kendrick* * *

White, everywhere white. And deep. And he was cold—so cold. He wondered how Father was doing in the northern territory—out in the open without walls and a fireplace.

Clearing a path to the barn, Kendrick used the only item in the house that would scoop snow. His hands were stiff and ached from the cold and his grip on the family shield grew difficult. He thought the ache must have been similar to his mother's pain.

He hoped to complete his task before the drifting snow filled in the trench—the wind drifted snow that hid behind obstructions and filled in low spots. Tears froze on his cheeks. He went back inside to warm his hands and feet.

Mother had advised Kendrick to stock pile wood inside the house at the first snowflake. Every couple of hours Kendrick would throw two logs on the fire. Mother would say, "Thank you, Kendrick." Except the last time— there had been no response.

As he paced the floor, and in alternate moments sat in a chair and cried, an hour passed. He had not prepared himself for this. The expectation of her death stretched out before him like a great valley. The range of his thoughts confused him—very sad she was gone, yet happy she was not in such misery.

Before her death, the disease had moved to her knees, elbows, shoulders, and jaw. She needed help to sit up the last three months; she'd had difficulty eating—he'd had to cut her food into very small pieces for her to swallow.

He avoided looking at her to keep his composure—he needed all his strength to complete his task. But he talked to her.

"This is the worst snow I can remember. And it is so cold. Worst you can remember too, I bet. We can say we shared this together. I was wondering how Father was doing out in the open. Oh, I will be another hour, or two."

He sat in a chair and held his bare feet toward the fire. His boots and gloves had been placed upside down on sticks nearby.

A few moments of warmth and the nerves started to function again. His feet and hands tingled as the cold released its grip. All his fingers and toes had good color.

His gloves and boots had stopped dripping. Kendrick needed to press on. He took his father's old shield outside to finish the path to the barn. For over an hour Kendrick knelt, gripped the shield's iced edge, plunged it into the hardening snow, scooped it toward himself, and emptied it downwind. Occasionally, he'd had to slap the shield with his hand when the snow stuck to it. Repeating this procedure escalated the ache in his joints.

Reaching the barn he was surprised that the goat was still alive and only one chicken had died. He built a shelf from stacked hay and returned to the house with some rope and the square wooden spade. The snow had stopped falling.

Before opening the door, he said, "Mother, I know you understand, you seemed to always read my mind. This is very difficult for me, but I must do this."

He went inside in control of his emotions. Although he knew it wasn't snow blindness, he wondered about his eyes. Thinking he saw Mother standing in the corner without the swollen and bumpy joints, she waved, and was gone.

He laid four short ropes on the floor, removed the twenty-year-old quilt she'd made before the swelling, and laid it on top of the ropes. Gently, he lifted Mother from the bed and placed her in the center of the blanket. He kissed her cheek.

"I love you. I already miss you."

Two sides of the blanket were laid over her, then the bottom. He looked at her for several minutes before folding the top that covered her face. The ropes were tied around the folded blanket.

Kendrick knelt, slid his arms under the blanket, and gently picked up his mother. Scooping the snow had exhausted his muscles, but he found the strength to carry her. He thought of the happy times they'd had together working the farm and the nights she read to him—and he remembered her smile.

He reached the barn and laid her softly on the stacked hay.

Kendrick stared at the bundled blanket. He left the barn focused on the ground and slowly walked the pathway in the snow, unaware of the cold.

* * *Oscar* * *

On their return to Manshire, the special Long Bow team had stopped at a burned out barn where the last remaining two walls stood slicing the wind around them. The horses were tied behind them to help retain the heat and keep the horses together. Huddled by the wind-swept fire, Oscar and twelve other Long Bows randomly felt the fire's heat tease them for a moment before the heat was swept by the relentless wind. The coals from the fire were constantly pushed to the center to keep the fire from dying. A couple of times they thought the wind had extinguished the fire. Several men were pale. If the storm did not stop soon, they would all perish.

It was time to find more wood—under normal conditions a difficult chore because the invaders had burned nearly all the wood close by.

Oscar took two of the healthier looking men with him to find wood. Their horses slipped and progressed slowly through the foot of snow. Turning their exposed faces from the pelting snow made guiding the horses around the mounds a challenge. A few hundred yards from their shelter, they found a small tree with an abundance of grey limbs. Oscar dismounted.

"Let me have your ropes," he said. "I want to snap this tree above the first limbs using our horses to break it. After the ropes are tied off here, tie them to our saddles. Three horses should be enough. When you hear the first snap, stop. We will reposition the horses to bring it completely down."

The Long Bows looked at each other and shrugged their shoulders.

Oscar caught their looks of disbelief while climbing the tree with his bare hands to tie the ropes at the right location. Completely exposed to the stinging snow carried by the wind, he wrapped the cold, stiff rope around the tree three times, and tied a bowline knot. He repeated the procedure for the other two ropes.

The ropes were tied around the high back to each armored saddle.

"The horses need to be about three feet apart and pulling together," Oscar said.

Nervously, the two Long Bows backed their horses. It reminded Oscar of the tug-a-war at the spring festival, but with a tree and three horses—and it was much colder. The loud crack had signaled their success and startled two deer about seventy feet down wind. All three men lifted their bows overhead. Three arrows silenced by the wind struck the front deer in the chest.

"Now, spread your horses about twenty feet apart. Repeat the tugging until the tree falls. Do not wait for me. Drag the tree back to our shelter. I will drag the deer to camp."

* * *

The early morning sun glistened off the snow. Everything was covered in a blanket of white. *A clean start*, Oscar thought. *Much like our conclusion with the invaders.*

He recalled the king's mission directive to stop the invaders. Also knew he must not let the coldness of the air, or his tired and weakening muscles stop him.

So it was that the next day he and the twelve Long Bows were off to gather information and return before the first snow, but this storm had come early.

Over forty days, they'd mapped locations destroyed by the invaders, collected samples, and traveled into Worchestor Province. If the situation presented itself, they would do some covert work to find out why the farms on both sides of the border had been attacked and destroyed.

The past Sunday, Oscar dressed like a commoner and entered the Worchestor Castle. The king and queen's meeting rooms were on the second floor, with the residence on the third floor. Oscar was surprised there were no guards posted on the second floor.

He knocked on the first door and waited for a response. No greeting, but he heard applause coming from down the hall. He felt safe in opening the door. It contained stored furniture and window panels. At the second door he placed his ear next to it. Just silence. He softly knocked.

A young girl's voice echoed through the hall, "Enter."

Oscar did not respond, and hoped there were no curious people in the second room.

He scanned the hallway looking for a safe hiding spot, but none was in sight. Oscar stepped to the hinge side of the doorway. If the door opened, he would hide behind it. Across the hall he saw the Worchestor flag painted on a door.

He started toward the flagged door as the second door opened slowly. Oscar peered through the gap to see a young girl, dressed in a white angel costume entering the hallway. She turned back into the room and said, "Come along. That knock was our signal to be on stage." Three girls walked down the hall dressed as angels. They left the door opened.

Oscar stepped across the hall—he'd found the king's meeting room. The large oak desk was to his left side in front of the heavy maroon drapes to hide the bare stonewalls. Paintings of the royal family were hung on the opposite wall. The floor was painted grey with a maroon border—the same colors as their flag. Two windows on the far wall provided the light during the daytime, and six oil lamps were placed throughout the office. He assumed the four chairs hung on the wall were pulled down as needed to visit the king.

Three stacks of papers were on the desk. One stack, face down, appeared to be completed—there were marks in the margins and some had been dog-eared. Another pile could not be categorized—drawings of what looked like an aqueduct, a couple of pages of poetry, a bound book, about thirty blank sheets, and some doodling of birds, flowers, and geometric patterns. The last stack had eleven sheets of paper with maps, a daily log, and a summary.

He read the summary.
Our initial findings lead us to believe that invaders from the south are behind the

burned farms. We discovered in our journey into Manshire that there were also burned out farms within their borders. Whoever is destroying these farms must be coming from the east. We have not found any survivors.

The map looked nearly identical to his map of landmarks and burned farms.

Voices grew louder in the hallway. The angels' door closed. He was about to hide behind the curtain, but the voices faded.

The handwriting was difficult to decipher on the daily log, but enough was readable to determine their findings matched Oscar's.

He walked to the office door listening for any sound in the hallway and opened the door slightly. It was clear. He stepped into the hallway, closed the door, walked ten feet, and encountered a guard coming from an intersecting hallway.

"Good morning," said the guard.

"Good morning," Oscar replied. "I have an appointment with the king tomorrow and wanted to find out where the meeting was."

"Interesting, King Emmanuel is preparing for his annual two-week hunting trip that starts tomorrow."

He thought about attempting to continue this charade and hope the guard did not call out for assistance. Or, *I could silence him now.*

In the next instant, he'd punched the guard near the bridge of his nose and turned to kick him in the abdomen. The clatter of the guard's shield and undrawn sword hitting the floor echoed in the long, straight hallways. Oscar walked quickly down the stairs then slowed slightly to avoid attention as he walked onto the street. A few civilians walked the cobblestone street toward the center of the village. Oscar knew he ought not to turn around to see what the current yelling was about.

He turned right after passing through the gate. There was no one in sight. He jogged to the corner on the inclined narrow patch of dirt between the wall and the moat. The standing moat water had a stale smell, and lacked the bubbling sounds of moving water he wished for to cover the splashing of small pebbles rolling under his feet. At the end of the wall, he turned right again, stopped to see if he was being`followed, then ran to his horse which was grazing along the wall.

The thundering sound of horses could be heard running across the drawbridge, just after the cathedral bell stuck the first of twelve gongs. Oscar kicked his horse and rode away from the castle. Dark clouds were moving swiftly from the west. He needed to gather his squad and ride hard toward Manshire.

* * *

Seven weeks and four days on a mission didn't seem so long after the baby exchange affair, Oscar thought. But it was nice to be back at Manshire Castle.

The majestic cut-stone castle sat atop the highest hill on the valley floor. From the north the large grey boulder field looked like the black freckles on his white horse. The river came from further north and meandered south until it reached the castle where it had been diverted around the southern side. The cathedral and village occupied the area around the castle from the river to the boulder field.

An orange sunset reflected off the diverted river sections that ran east or west. It was a beautiful setting worthy of all efforts to protect it.

After the horses were stabled, a dinner in the main hall preceded a night's sleep in the barracks.

The following morning, Oscar reported to the king. It began just as it had always begun, with trivial but necessary words.

"Good morning Oscar. Good to have you back. Tell me about your investigation."

"Good morning, my king. The area from the farthest north of Manshire into Worchester shows signs of attack along the border between the two countries. Documentation in their king's meeting room indicated Worchester thought we were the invaders."

"Are the Worchester farm attacks similar?"

"Yes, the homes, chicken coops, and barns are burned out. So far, there are no survivors to talk to—all have been burned in the house or the barn. The large animals are burned, but there is evidence the small animals are taken for food by the invaders. Any footprints, hooved prints, and wagon tracks were washed away by rain and snow."

"Could the Worchester attacks be a ruse?"

"Not likely. The invaders have struck Worchester more frequently. Like here, the invaders attacks are seasonal, late spring through early autumn, and they are using the heavily forested areas for cover.

"How do you know they are seasonal?" the king asked.

"There are burned fruit and leaf stems on the trees, and ashes from the burned gardens.

"Should we camp a group to gather more information and monitor the border?" the king asked.

"Placing a team in May for six months might be worth the effort."

"Plan to send a five man observation team in early April."

Big and Ugly

The crisp air continued to tickle her cheeks—a couple of sneezes were suppressed by pinching her nose. The aromatic steam rising from the loaves of bread, the enriched color of vegetables harvested in recent days, and the animated antics of merchants and customers bargaining filled her with joy—*yes, these were real, proud people*. They'd survived the harsh freezing winter, the endless dark days of spring rain, and summer's oppressive humid heat. Their contagious smiles floated through the market on the gentle breeze.

But not all was perfect. The cumbersome unavoidable clothing layers made the sweat accumulate at the small of her back. The salt-stained dress would be hard to hide from Father—unless she returned earlier than planned. The material repeatedly peeled slowly from her back with each child, cart, or basket that bumped her from behind.

Still, that was the least of her worries. Her father's health and the hint of a conspiracy were ever more troubling. But alone at the market she was free to think.

"Halt! ... I say Halt!"

Thud!

Faster than she turned toward the command, someone had knocked her to the ground. *She was caught. No. They wouldn't hurt her.* "Flaming dragons!" she cried.

The blurred figure of a man running away preceded the pain. The tenderized bump started to protrude across her forehead.

"Are you all right, miss?" asked a merchant.

"I think so, thank you," she replied.

"Let me help you get off the ground before the market tramples you into the cobblestones. That's a nasty bump. Here, sit on this crate until you are ready to go."

She watched two men running through the crowd until they disappeared from view. Althea touched the bump on her forehead. *How was she going to hide this from Father?*

"Who hit me?" she asked.

"A thief," he replied. "And he is about to meet Kendrick, the self-proclaimed sheriff of Manshire Province market. He is actually quite good at protecting us from thieves and pickpockets. We need protection from his boisterous, bragging nature."

The clamor of the market filled the air once again.

"Is he always here?"

"Yes, lately. He thinks he is a master at hiding, but if you look closely you can catch him crouching behind the merchants' carts."

"I thought that was just a young beggar."

"Kendrick is both a blessing and a curse. It is difficult to understand his motives. But I can assure you he is quite self-sufficient. He never expects or takes the food we offer him."

"Where can I find this scallywag? I wish to talk to the thief that ran me over."

"Shhh ... Here he comes."

Even the most delicate head movements hastened the pain. She twisted her body in the direction of the merchant's gaze—*much better.*

"Are you all right, miss?" Kendrick asked.

"I seem to have developed a painful bump," she replied. Her hand gently rubbed the bruise as if she expected it to disappear by her touch. "Did you catch him?"

"Yes, I am returning the coin bag he lifted from the butcher." He pointed to a cart about thirty feet away. "He will not be returning to Manshire."

"How can you be sure?"

Kendrick tossed the butcher's coin purse in his right hand. "I threatened to break his hand if he returned. I am not one to be taken lightly." He paused. "I have seen you around, but you never buy anything. Nothing gets by me in *my* market. What is your name?" Kendrick asked.

"Althea," she replied as she removed her hand from the bump. "So, this is *your* market?"

Her eyes seemed familiar. The bruise was irresistible. He had to touch it.

"Have we met before? What is your family name?" Kendrick asked as he lightly touched the darkening bruise.

She flinched uncomfortably, "No. We have not met." The reply was quick. "What are you doing?" *Couldn't he just forget about the bump?*

"It is so big and ugly," he said.

She stood and swayed a couple times placing her hand on the cart's edge. She rubbed her temple with the other hand.

Kendrick moved to catch her.

"Oh, you —" She staggered away.

Althea was glad Kendrick couldn't read her mind for she found him immature, egotistical, and a boaster. She would have been happier talking to a frog. But still, something about him intrigued her.

* * *

She followed the soft center ribbon of brown grass between the earthen ruts.

Althea couldn't help it, but she missed the daily market. Now, her weekly escape was to the surrounding countryside. The slight increase in temperature served as warning that snow would soon blanket the ground. As she strolled, shuttered windows and cords of split wood near the entrance of the country homes announced winter's approach. Althea wished the warm smoke billowing from the chimneys would brush by her cold cheeks.

It'd been two full moons since her encounter with the self-proclaimed sheriff, Kendrick. Her gloved hand touched the spot of the former bruise she managed to hide from Father with make-up and a new-jeweled hairstyle.

Frustration and intrigue were part of her personal life. One moment she was angry with Kendrick because she could not get him out of her mind, and just as rapidly she would be anticipating their second meeting.

Occasionally, she was lost pondering in Manshire Province. These weekly escapes helped develop her sense of wellbeing. They helped her to prepare for the responsibilities that would one day be hers.

Lately, her thoughts were focused on Father's coughing from the depths of his chest. Blood had come up a few weeks ago during an extended episode. And adding to her troubles was her younger brother's frequent and mysterious trips to the archbishop. Her efforts to discuss Father's condition were ignored with her brother's cold detachment.

She adjusted her coat tighter around her neck and shoulders. Just as she reached for her scarf, there appeared from nowhere, ruffians.

"What have we here?" said the tall husky leader. He wore a grey scarf over his mouth and nose.

Althea screamed.

"It looks like a noble lady. No, a *lost* noble lady," said another ruffian.

"We have been following you for a long time. You are lost. We're not. We know there are no houses close. Salty," he asked his associate, "are you cold? I'm cold—that coat would be nice and warm. Does that coat come with a money pocket?"

"You will have to pry this coat from me. It's a gift from my father, King Louis III," Althea said. She knew she had made a mistake, but she had to do something.

Laughter erupted

The tall ruffian nodded to Salty and they smiled.

Althea took advantage of the ruffians whispering amongst themselves. The tall ruffian said, "I am sure it's her."

Her heart pounded as she stepped backwards and continued to scan for the right weapon. In the assortment of limbs and branches littering the ground, she picked up a sturdy five-foot stick with a splintered end, which she kept pointed at her attackers.

She was glad the tree's canopy provided shade from the moonlight. Its wide trunk made it difficult for the ruffians to locate her silhouette.

"Hey, she is moving away," said the short ruffian.

They moved near her.

"Salty, pry the coat from her," said the tall-husky-leader.

Salty lunged at her. In that second, Althea thrust the splintered end toward Salty's midsection. He dodged the stick, but his arm received several cuts.

"Lady, do you think you can fight all five of us? We want your coat, your money, and your—." The leader's speech was cut off as he gasped for breath. He clutched his chest. Pain evidenced on his distorted face. From the darkness behind the trunk came an unknown man whose feet had struck him chest high.

The mystery man yanked the stick from Althea's hands. Red cuts appeared on Salty's cheeks. Blood began to flow. Instinct told her to take the stick as it appeared in front of her. Shock best described her recognition of the mystery man.

"Kendrick!"

"Please do not hit me," Kendrick said.

The tall leader was bent over. He clutched at his chest as he ran away.

"Here is how I see this," he said to the ruffians. "It is the four of you against me; your leader has left you. Odds are in my favor. So, do you want to walk away as you are, or painfully bruised? Another thought occurs to me, you could die here. Do you have a preference on which side of the tree to be buried?"

Confusion showed on two of the three ruffians' faces—one had red hair, the other had a scraggly beard. Self-preservation appeared on the short one's face.

The redhead widened his stance. His nostrils flared with each deep breath like the bellows heating the coals at the livery stable. Kendrick felt the heat from the red head's breath as he blocked the punch. A slight push with his blocking arm exposed the red head's back. Kendrick summoned all his energy and struck him in the kidneys.

Kendrick somersaulted toward the bearded man. He came to his feet and punched him in the nose. The bearded man landed on his back.

"Do you wish to be buried here?" he asked the short ruffian.

"No."

"Then collect your friends and leave Manshire Province." Kendrick looked around and the tall-husky-leader was gone.

Less than the time required for a leaf to fall, the fighting ended. Kendrick turned to her. Althea reminded him of a statue until a smile broke her petrified face.

"Where did you learn to do that?" Althea asked.

"My father taught me," Kendrick replied. "Would you like to stay here? The village is three-hours away. Or, would you like me to escort you back to your home? Or, you can come home with me—a short mile walk."

"Will dinner be served at your home?" she asked.

"Rabbit stew."

"What will your parents say?"

"Mother passed away and Father is working in the north territory."

Her pulse quickened. She swallowed to cure her dry throat.

"What will your wife say when you bring me home?"

"I am not married."

She adjusted her coat and looked down at her buttons to hide her smile.

* * *

Althea held the torch while Kendrick dug up the potatoes and carrots he'd buried in a clay pot for winter. He milked the goat and selected two apples from the barrel. The torch cast strange shadows while Kendrick worked, but it warmed her. In the house, her chin rested in cupped hands. She watched with amazement while Kendrick carved the rabbit meat and prepared the vegetables. Water splashed from the pot as the ingredients were added. "You are really quite good in the kitchen," she said.

"Thank you. My mother would be proud to hear that."

The fire warmed the small home and cast an orange glow on everything. Kendrick moved the coals around and placed fresh firewood on top. The pot was placed on the hook then pushed over the fire. "It will be ready in about an hour."

"The short days of winter depress me," she said. "A few moons ago, we were enjoying the autumn breeze and watching the sunset after dinner."

"Winter is the time to rest, plan, and prepare for summer. The snow covers everything like a blanket and challenges us to plan how we will use the gifts while nature is resting. Each season prepares us for the next."

His words were a bit more wise and thoughtful than she'd expected from a farmer's son. She liked that about him. "I hadn't thought of it that way, but it makes sense," she said.

"Yes. Everything is connected. The stars, moon, sun, weather, seasons, and so on."

"How is policing the market connected?" she asked.

"I protect the market to sharpen my skills. My dream is to become a Long Bow. I want to protect Manshire Province from invaders. Hopefully, the Long Bows will hear of me through my sheriff duties. Why do you attend the market and yet never buy?"

"Mostly, I enjoy the activity. I have no money to buy."

About an hour later, Kendrick set the hand carved twin prong forks and spoons on the table.

She asked, "What happened to your mother?"

Kendrick tasted the stew. "Good." He spooned it into bowls cut and carved from a tree trunk. He placed the apples carefully on the fresh logs. "I bought some cinnamon at the market last summer. It is very tasty on warm apples. I hope you like it."

"Your mother?" she persisted.

"Mother had joint problems. They got so bad she was bedridden the last few months. She lived with it for a long time—too long she suffered. She died last winter. I stored her body in the barn—buried her in the spring when the ground thawed, under that big tree you fought at today."

He stored the body in the barn? She thought. *It sounds so gruesome ... maybe not ... the morning frost has hardened the earthen roads.*

"I am sorry," she said.

Kendrick finished his stew and prepared the apples. Althea's eyes widened, and she took several deep breaths of the pleasing aroma before she tasted the seasoned apples. "This is wonderful."

* * Kendrick * *

Their conversation continued for another hour. Kendrick assumed the day's activities had tired Althea. As she struggled to stay awake, she would jerk just before she fell asleep. He continued to talk about his plans to purchase his aunt and uncle's old farm, become a Long Bow, and buy a horse, until she slept. Kendrick placed her in the bed and covered her.

The aging wooden hinges creaked. When the opening was wide enough Kendrick slipped passed the door. Quickly he closed the door to keep the cold air from waking her. A few split logs were repositioned on the wood stack to make a bed where he would watch his favorite constellations.

The moon's absence let the stars' brilliance contrast with the dark reaches of the universe. Tonight was a gift from the stars as Draco the dragon and Pegasus the winged horse shone particularly bright.

He was atop Pegasus when he heard a maiden scream.

The sound was like a large screech owl.

Pegasus followed the sound.

A man with a small stride avoided the sizeable fallen limbs to catch the maiden.

She wore two dresses and a tattered coat—too many layers hampered her escape.

A man grabbed her shoulder as they ran, then held her arms to keep her still.

They fell and were quickly surrounded by several men.

Kendrick leapt from atop Pegasus like an acrobat in the market.

He kicked one man, spun and kicked a second, while Pegasus kicked two men with his hind legs.

Another shrill scream called to Kendrick.

He flung his family shield at the man between him and the maiden.

Retrieving his shield, he ran to free her. With a push, the kidnapper released her and shot an arrow toward Kendrick.

It ricocheted off the shield...

Funny, his dreams were more like visions of being invincible, fearless, and respected. True life was usually the opposite.

He opened his eyes. The morning brought a light snow that tickled his nose and forehead.

Suddenly, a scream. Several logs thumped Kendrick before he rose from the ground.

The door lever cleared the catch. It flew open under Kendrick's weight.

"Flaming dragons!" he heard her cry. "I am going to have another bruise in that same spot."

"Are you all right? I am sorry. I heard you scream and thought you were in danger."

"Waking up in a strange house scared me. I apologize for being a girl."

"For a girl, you stood your ground with those men quite well last night."

"Thank you for the compliment, I think."

"You are welcome. Can I interest you in boiled potatoes for breakfast?"

"Yes, thank you." She rubbed the knot on her forehead.

In a strange way, getting her head bruised every time they were together was funny. But he must not laugh. It would be unkind. She would walk away mad again.

"The wolves will be out today. Last night's snow will drive the deer down for easier food. I will walk you home."

* * *

Kendrick looked at Althea as she walked backwards to look at the two sets of footprints in the snow. From her expression he assumed she saw things with a fresh view. He turned and walked backwards. She smiled at him.

Kendrick stopped walking. He placed a hand on her forearm.

"What are you doing?" she asked.

Kendrick placed a finger at his lips. "Quiet please. I hear something unusual."

For a few seconds they stood still. Kendrick could see Althea shaking from the cold. He handed her his coat.

"I can hear it too," she whispered.

"I am concerned they might be invaders from the north. We must hide, there, behind those large boulders."

The thunder of several horses racing towards them grew louder.

Crouching, Kendrick peered over the boulders. The only footprints in the snow led directly to their location.

"If these men are marauders or invaders, I will hold them off after diverting them down the road. As soon as they pass, you run over this hill and ask the Hamiltons for refuge. Tell them I sent you. Do not stop until you are safe."

Before she spoke, Kendrick had disappeared.

His boots slipped on the snow as he tried to run faster. The thunder grew louder, faster. He glanced at the passing horseman then down to the crest on the blanket. Immediately, he knew his capture was imminent. He slid to the edge of the road breathing heavily as he placed his hands on his knees. He waited for the horsemen to finish surrounding him before he stood up. Their horses produced steam as they exhaled.

"Hello, Father," Kendrick said, upon recognizing him.

"Kendrick, why are you running?" Oscar asked.

"I thought you were invaders returning to the north," he replied. "I wanted to divert you from a maiden I sent over the hill to hide from you."

"What is the maiden's name?" his father asked.

Kendrick hesitated—perhaps the pause was too long.

"Kendrick! You are trying my patience. What is the maiden's name?"

"Althea."

In unison the knights slapped their swords, startling Kendrick.

Oscar raised his hand to relax the knights.

"Where can we find Althea?"

"She went over the hill." He pointed toward the Hamiltons.

Instantly, Oscar looked troubled. Kendrick saw a new expression from his father.

"Sergeant, let him ride with you."

Kendrick and the sergeant locked arms. Kendrick prepared to mount the horse behind the sergeant. "Wait! I hear yelling."

"Kendrick! Kendrick!" Althea was waving her arms over her head.

The sergeant's confused look amused Kendrick. "Well, go and get her," he said.

The sergeant tugged on the reins and kicked the horse in the haunches. Near Althea, he dismounted the horse to let her ride in the saddle. Another horseman left the circle to pick up the sergeant who mounted the back of the moving horse in a single motion.

She patted the horse's neck. "Good girl."

"Princess Althea, are you all right?" Oscar inquired.

"Yes captain, I am safe. Thanks to Kendrick. He saved me from a mugging, fed me, and guarded the house while I slept." She winked at Kendrick, then dusted the snow off her coat.

"Princess, where did you get that bruise?"

"In the scuffle with the ruffians." She reached up to touch the bump. "Captain, can we take this gallant young man back to his home before we return to the castle?"

"Kendrick is my son and lives a couple miles up this road. I am sure he will be fine. We need to return you to the castle. The king will be worried."

She rolled her eyes.

Oscar circled his hand in the air and the knights fell into formation. Althea pulled the reins to the right, and the horse ambled to Kendrick. She leaned in the saddle as she returned his coat. "Kendrick, I watched the horses gallop by. I recognized the crest," she offered for his unspoken question. "So, you are Oscar's son. I am sorry for not telling you my father is the king. I so enjoyed your company, dinner, and our walk this morning. I hope to see you again soon."

Kendrick held her hand for a few moments before he kissed it. His heart beat a little faster and he blushed remembering the excitement they'd shared together—the thief in the market, the ruffians under the big tree, digging up the clay pot, cinnamon apples, walking backwards in the snow, and two bruises.

"Goodbye Althea. I too, enjoyed our time together." He smiled.

"Goodbye Kendrick," she said, tugging the reins and leaving him. He watched until they were out of sight.

On the walk home Kendrick could see the footprints they'd created and he wondered where he'd first seen those icy blue eyes.

Cinnamon Apples

The week of spring's beginning meant time to plow and feel the good earth. Plant the garden. Feed the soil. Trim the fruit trees. Kendrick's painful blisters served as a reminder that the reward for his labor would feed Father and him through next winter.

Two doves cooed and occasionally fluttered— attempting escape from his trap. *Killing these birds in early spring—seemed like a stab at nature.* A deep breath of fresh spring air filled his lungs. The doves gentle calling beckoned as he unlatched the trap's door. A surprise rewarded his actions—the doves appeared to bow as they walked from the trap—they flew together seconds later. It would be another dinner of roots.

There was another surprise as Kendrick passed the bushes in the path's curve. The last person Kendrick expected to visit was napping in a chair leaning against the house. Just a hundred feet away, Kendrick noticed the man's left eye was open.

"Good afternoon, sergeant," Kendrick said.

"And a fine spring afternoon it is," said the sergeant of the Long Bows. He stood and stretched his arms.

"What brings you this far from the castle?"

"I have been appointed to be the princess's escort. A duty I am thankful to you for. At her command, I have been instructed to deliver this note to only you."

The sergeant handed the envelope to Kendrick. He saw the stamped wax seal.

"Sergeant, I have roots for dinner. You are welcome to stay the night."

"I am tempted to stay if you are having cinnamon apples. They are now a new item on the castle's regular dinner offerings."

"Sorry, I am out of apples and cinnamon."

The sergeant whistled. His horse stopped grazing and walked to him. "Just as well," the sergeant said. "Kendrick, she asked that I tell you. The castle is in conflict. The king's health is concerning her. She needs a confidant." The sergeant paused as if he were deciding to reveal more. "I must return before the Long Bows send a search party for me." He mounted his horse.

"Understood. Please tell Althea hello."

Anticipation gave Kendrick a nervous stomach. He wanted desperately to open the note, but waited until the sergeant had disappeared beyond the curve.

Kendrick slid his knife under the flap's fold and carefully removed the note.

Dear Kendrick,

The winter moon's patient meandering had me guessing if spring would ever arrive. Alas, it's here.

I miss you and our brief time together. I miss your fresh point of view. Spring's arrival has truly become a time of struggle for Father and I.

Please meet me below the Crimson Cliffs at the grand curve of Dover Creek two miles north of the castle, three mornings hence. Remember to bring some of those delicious cinnamon apples.

126

Cheers,

Althea

* * *

Kendrick attempted to hasten the meeting by keeping busy with spring chores. But it did not work.

On the third day, he awoke early. He gathered two eggs from the chicken coop and scrambled them with roots and early spring berries. They were not as good as Mother's omelets.

The beauty of spring escaped his awareness as he walked. *How must he address her? What courtesies must he observe? Who else will be present when we talk?*

An eagle's cry aroused his attention. His anxious nerves quieted as the eagle gently glided on the currents. The jumble of questions evaporated from his mind. The eagle screeched again. In that moment, his purpose was clear—protect Althea.

Gathering the sack he ran toward the grand curve. As he crested the last hill of his journey, the Crimson Cliffs' brilliant color brought out the deep green of the forest; designed by God like a grand amphitheater, it's very shape prevented someone from spying on conversations. The trees' canopy hid the forest floor. A narrow canyon controlled both entrance points. This location had been chosen on purpose.

It was the area surrounding the grand curve that could be more important. Where could he take Althea if trouble should find them? Where could he hide her in plain sight?

One hundred twenty yards from the entrance, Kendrick crouched behind a raspberry vine. He watched for birds that might give away their escape. *There! What was that unusual movement? There! Again. It was a knight hiding in the wild lavender. Didn't he know bees liked the purple blossoms? The birds had already flown away.*

Kendrick stood, raised his sack above his head and approached the sentry.

"Halt, who goes there?"

"I am Kendrick."

"What is the password?"

Password! Oh, a password. It must have been in the envelope. No, he'd looked in the envelope—only the note. It must be in the note. Winter's moon ... spring's arrival ... Crimson Cliffs ... ah, yes ...

"Cinnamon apples."

"Enter Kendrick. She is waiting for you by the flat rock at the stream. Three hundred yards that way." The sentry pointed with his long bow to Kendrick's left.

Kendrick continued to analyze locations for hiding.

* * *Althea* * *

The disguised Althea as a Long Bow knight in leather pants, cotton long-sleeved shirt, feathered hat, wool cape, and weapons surprised him. Her deliberate pacing revealed a troubled soul. She focused on the fresh path. To her right, two Long Bows rode horses and three other horses grazed.

Kendrick walked toward her. The Long Bows positioned their horses between Althea and Kendrick as they drew their swords. "Halt!"

"Cinnamon apples," Kendrick said.

Althea walked to the front of the horses. She looked at Kendrick, then to the two Long Bows.

"It is he." She said nodding to the horsemen, "Please wait over there," and pointed to an area further into the forest.

A smile replaced her concerned look. She continued after the horsemen were at a safe distance—safe for protection and safe for privacy. "By the way, there is no password here, as I know who you are. Thank you for coming, Kendrick. I have missed you."

"It is nice to see you again. I too, have missed you."

She gestured to her right then walked in that direction. Kendrick followed for about fifteen yards.

"This has become my sanctuary. I can no longer go to the market or roam the countryside. Father's health has become public, and everyone knows of me as the next queen of Manshire Province," she said. "Once a week I come here to think. Please remove your shoes. I want you to enjoy dangling your feet in the cool stream."

Kendrick helped Althea remove her shoes. He saw the birthmark on her left sole. She sat on the flat rock's edge. Kendrick joined her.

"This is very nice. I could get used to this," Kendrick replied.

Althea looked ahead for a few minutes.

"What are we permitted to discuss?" Kendrick asked.

"If you ask something I wish to keep private, I will tell you."

"Very well. How is the king?"

She turned to Kendrick. A tear rolled over her cheek. She wiped it.

"I am afraid his health is not good. He digresses daily."

"What is his ailment?"

"Consumption. It started twenty-two months ago with a persistent mild cough. It appeared to be aggravated by the cold weather.

Again, she gazed forward and wiped another tear with her right hand.

"What treatment has he had?"

"Father is one to exhaust all the options. He has had various shaman administer their potions and herbs, cast spells, and perform incantations. He has asked the archbishop to pray for him—which is bold, or desperate, to ask of a presumed enemy. Last week he coughed up blood, again."

"How are you?"

"I am so busy learning the affairs of state, I have not had time to think much about myself. Kendrick, I want to talk with you, but can we spend today in silence?"

"Certainly."

Althea leaned her head on Kendrick's shoulder. A moment later, she napped.

While she rested, he noticed two flat red stones in the rippling stream.

Five minutes passed until she whispered, "Thank you."

"You are welcome. What else can I do for you?"

"Meet me here every week."

"I am honored to fulfill your wish."

"Kendrick, another wish I would like you to consider. The Knight Games are approaching. This would be a splendid opportunity to garner some favor from Father."

A nervous delight raced through his body and his heart pounded.

"I have heard of them. Father would not let me attend. What happens? How do they work?" A spice of the boisterous Kendrick could be heard in his voice.

"It is also important that you be you. Father would not have much patience with the *market sheriff* Kendrick. There are four events. Participants receive scores based on individual events and the total of all events. Events include knife throwing, an obstacle course, running, and archery. Three challengers are given approval by the king to participate. If a challenger places in the top five he can join the Long Bows. Because the king is my father, I can arrange your approval."

* * *Kendrick* * *

Two days later, it was an hour until sunset and the long shadows of the castle covered a majority of the market. The merchants were making their best deals and closing up. It was a typical late afternoon crowd, mostly customers looking for a bargain. A short, young man dipped, slid, ducked, and generally ran through the market. Only thirty feet from Kendrick, he stole a loaf of bread, grabbed a shirt, and two apples from three adjacent carts.

Kendrick, annoyed by the thief, gave chase. The short man moved through the crowd with ease after stealing the two apples. Kendrick struggled to move through the crowd. Thoughts of Althea distracted his heart. He had come today specifically hoping she might make a rare disguised appearance. He assumed the thief slowed from poor conditioning. In spite of his struggle, Kendrick closed the distance between them.

Kendrick was only ten feet away and preparing to grab the thief as he received his second wind. In the crowd, the short man had increased the distance between them, stealing a pair of gloves as he ran by the cart. Kendrick assumed Althea would not come out after this disturbance, and gave his full concentration to the chase.

Kendrick reduced the distance quickly after both men had exited the market. As Kendrick was about to tackle him, the short man changed directions running between two buildings. Kendrick over-ran the alley and had to circle around.

Surprised by how close he was to the short man when he passed through the alley, Kendrick ran faster, risking a collision with a tree. He struggled to maintain his balance. Reaching up he felt the bleeding, sore spot as another rock hit his side, taking him down.

* * Oscar * *

Oscar wandered through the market looking for his son. He had wanted to discuss Abbey's death with him for weeks but had never been sure how to bring it up. So he hoped a talk about Althea might open the opportunity to discuss Abbey's death. He would start with two days ago; he had seen Althea dressed as a Long Bow riding with four of his men.

He asked the merchants if they had seen Kendrick. Gathering information was like crossing a stream one stone at a time, as the merchants could direct him to the next merchant, but not to where he was now. Oscar exited the crowd into the area for hauling services, blacksmith, and warehousing. As he passed the blacksmith shop, he looked down the alley.

In an instant, Oscar ran and withdrew an arrow from his quiver. A volley of rocks rained on Kendrick.

The slight incline of the grassy ground ended at the river's edge—fifty feet below the reentry of the diversion that created the moat. A few young pine trees were scattered among the clusters of tall wild rose bushes; willows thickened closer to the river.

At the end of the alley, Oscar stopped. The rocks came from behind a semicircle of five bushes. He determined the position of the first two men watching the rocks paths. Estimating the position of the first man, he released an arrow through the rose bush at the visible spots of his yellow shirt. The man yelled painfully.

The second arrow required a higher degree of estimating as the bush grew slightly behind the first one. Half of the faint silhouette shown through the branches, and a voice coming from the bush asked, "Salty, are you there?" Oscar released arrow number two. A man with a scraggly beard fell without a sound from behind the bush onto the thick grass.

When the rocks stopped, a man with red hair appeared from behind a boulder. He ran at Kendrick, a large stick held above his head. He was about to strike Kendrick when an arrow entered his shoulder. The stick fell from his hands. The red headed man sat against a tree. Oscar pulled the string a little farther and released an arrow. The arrowhead sliced through the same shoulder and buried itself in the soft, young pine tree. Oscar did not want a repeat of the attempted kidnapping. He wanted someone to interrogate.

Only three arrows left.

With arrow and bow ready to position, he approached Kendrick to assess his condition. Crouching, he slowly stepped across the grass moving his eyes frequently between the cover and Kendrick. The slightest nuance in the background would receive his full attention. A spider web reflected light as it twisted in the wind. Ducking as he passed it, he heard a rock hit a tree behind him. They had given away their position.

"I am the captain of the Long Bows. Surrender and I will spare your life."

A dull muffled thud broke the silence.

He advanced toward the thud—more cautious than before.

Kendrick moaned. Moments later he was quiet.

Instantly, Oscar broke into a full run until he'd reached the edge of the bushes. One short man lay dead. He had been struck in the head. A bloody stone lay next to him. He scanned the ground and found footprints running away from the ambush.

Oscar returned to Kendrick. The large bruise on his forehead was bleeding. There were multiple bruises on his left side and nothing on his right side. Oscar slapped Kendrick's right cheek. "Wake up son. We still have lots to do together."

Kendrick reached up. "I hurt all over."

"You were stoned."

"I was ambushed."

"Someone wants you dead." Oscar struggled with the thought his boy was a target, and all his efforts had not kept him from the business of the monarchy. Oscar needed to confirm his suspicions. His life would be aimless if he lost Kendrick so close to Abbey.

"Are you still seeing Althea?" Oscar asked.

"Um, yes. But who would want me dead? Help me up."

Kendrick stood as Father steadied him.

"Lean against this tree. I need to check on our prisoner."

"Prisoner?"

"I stuck him to that tree." Oscar pointed to a tree behind Kendrick.

Kendrick blinked, taking the man in. "I know this guy. He's one of the ruffians that tried to mug Althea the night before you rescued her."

"Kendrick, lean on me. I need you look at this other bandit." They walked a short distance. "Do you recognize him?" Oscar asked.

"Yes, that's the bearded ruffian. I think this other man is Salty."

"Son, you have aroused someone's attention. And, your relationship with the princess has been noticed. I think these men were out to assassinate the princess when you first encountered them. We need to gather more information."

Kendrick stumbled from tree to tree. Oscar prepared to interrogate the prisoner. He removed his knife and made a point of twisting it back and forth.

The redheaded man's eyes followed the knife.

"What is your name?" Oscar asked.

"Martin."

"Martin, this is going to hurt. I am going to tell you in great detail so you can prepare for the pain."

Martin stared into the forest.

"First I am going to pull you away from this tree. The second anchor arrow holding you to this tree will slide through your shoulder. I do this for your benefit, so I can cut the head off the first arrow with this knife. The first arrowhead is partially through the shoulder. I apologize, because I have to push it through to cut the arrowhead off. After I slide the shaft back through the wound, we can stop the bleeding from the first arrow."

Martin looked resolved. It appeared he would not give Oscar any satisfaction.

"Now if you can sit there without moving, the anchor will not hurt, much! But Martin, you look tired, scared, and weak. I am guessing you will experience many sharp pains in your attempt to be still and will perceive these pains to be worse than sliding back along the anchor's shaft. You will decide to slide down the shaft. I warn you that either decision will be very painful."

Martin's jaw was set. Muscles flexed about his chin.

"Or I can reduce the total pain and cut the anchor arrow off while you are leaning forward. To help you with your decision, let me touch the first arrow."

Oscar flipped the first arrow with his index finger. Martin let out a painfully long scream. He breathed deeply and rapidly while the pain subsided.

"Martin, you need another test?"

"NO, NO, *please* NO!"

"Whom are you working for?"

"A spy we call him, Skinny. We were hired help and were to be paid after the job was done."

Oscar prepared to flip the arrow again. Martin's eyes were fully open alternating between Oscar's finger and eyes.

"Really. Honest. *I speak the truth.*"

"What was your objective that night under the big oak?" Kendrick asked.

"We were sent to kidnap her."

"Who sent you?" Kendrick moved toward Martin.

Not wanting Kendrick to interfere with the interrogation's rhythm, Oscar placed his hand on Kendrick's shoulder and tilted his head away from Martin.

Kendrick backed away.

"Who paid your leader?" Oscar asked.

"We just called him Skinny. It is rumored he is a spy."

"Spy from where?"

* * *

Oscar escorted Kendrick to the king's hunting cabin, a spacious two-floor log building with two large windows on each side of the main door. Four chimneys rose above the roofline.

"Kendrick, you can stay here for a few days to recover from your injuries."

Oscar removed the blankets from the furniture.

"Will you get in trouble for using this?"

"Yes. But, it is not hunting season, and the king has not used this for years since losing the first boy.

"Can you retrieve my sack from behind the bush at the side wagon gate?"

Get some rest while I go round up some supper. I will retrieve your sack."

* * *

That night, the familiar smell of rabbit cooking stirred Kendrick from sleep.

"How do you feel?" Oscar asked. He sat Kendrick's sack on the floor.

"Better. Still stiff on my left side."

"That will go away in a few days. You need to eat."

"Thanks for getting my weapons sack."

Kendrick limped to the table, eased himself into the chair, and rummaged through the sack while waiting.

"My knife is missing."

"Are you sure? Check again," Oscar asked as he prepared the dinner in the wood burning brick oven.

"It's missing. It's the one you and mother gave me that I made the scabbard for it."

"The one you carved '*Family*' onto the leather?"

"Yes."

"When are you going to start carrying your weapons for use? They are not toys to be put away in a sack."

"Wish I had them with me yesterday."

Oscar brought two plates to the table. "We don't have time for the knife anyway," he began. "If Martin is correct, you should continue to meet with Althea. She needs someone who can listen to her. We could always use her smart analysis. Talking will comfort her and will help formulate ideas and solutions."

Dinner finished, Oscar was about to clean up the dishes, a task primarily reserved for his wife, when Kendrick asked, "Father, we have not had time to talk about Mother's passing."

To be sure, it was the question Oscar had been dreading for some weeks now, ever since he'd stood by the mound of earth and told his beloved his good-byes. What would he tell his son now? How would he get through it? Where would he begin? What could he possibly share with his son that might curb the aching feeling he hadn't been able to shrug away from his own heart.

"I know," Oscar said, "but son..."

A small tear was already caressing the boy's left cheek. "I know Father."

"Your mother and I met on a country road, did you know that? The axel had broken on her overloaded wagon. Your grandfather and I helped repair the axel, which as you know, takes several hours. She was seventeen and quite a talker. They settled a few miles away and I would visit her once or twice a month."

Kendrick had his elbow on the table. Now, he leaned into his cupped hand, tears falling through his fingers. His gaze never left his father's.

"Our conversations covered everything from farming to raising children. I was impressed with her desire to make the world a better place each day. She was full of life." He stopped a moment and looked up to the ceiling, then continued. "We could talk about anything, including my joining the Long Bows. She understood the need for laws and enforcement—a decision I have second-guessed a few times. We could have spent more time together."

His eyes were wet, and he blinked a few times to clear them.

"She had such a positive attitude about her disease, except the one time we found her crying in the garden. I miss her. She was my queen." Oscar leaned back in the chair.

"My last moment with her," Kendrick began, "I had returned to the house after clearing a path through the snow. I think I saw her spirit leaving—her joints looked normal, and she waved." Kendrick looked away. Oscar knew he was hiding tears from him; tears he had already seen. "I miss her, but I'm happy she is not suffering anymore."

* *Kendrick* * *

For the past three days, Kendrick had rested in the king's cabin. At the market, a wound on his upper cheek and forehead had brought him more attention than he'd wished for. Sympathy, greetings, and thanks offered him calmed his sense of urgency. He *was* home.

Kendrick decided to split his attention between the market and the castle. For the first time since his sheriff duties had begun, he'd searched for unusual activities around the castle. Walking through the crowd helped to cover his frequent passes by the side wagon gate in the castle's wall.

Twice today, he'd noticed the lad walking out a castle door, through the wagon gate, crossing the street, and spending time in the cathedral.

Oddly, the sergeant of the Long Bows sat in the sun next to his saddled horse while the other Long Bows practiced archery, swordplay, and hand–to–hand combat.

* * *

On the fourth day since leaving his father's home, at least for a time, Kendrick rose from bed early to spend extra time in the grand curve. He needed to be thoroughly familiar with the area. He found three locations for hiding Althea if necessary. He stashed a sword at his preferred location, and a knife Father had loaned him as a second choice.

Satisfied he had emergency options, he'd left her sanctuary to watch the Long Bows security measures from the hill. Althea and four Long Bows entered the far end of the grand curve area. Kendrick waited for them to establish their security precautions.

"Halt, who goes there?"

"It is I, Kendrick. Cinnamon apples."

"Same location," the sentry said.

The horsemen drew their swords as Kendrick entered from behind the bushes.

"Put your swords away," Althea commanded. "Wait over there. Thank you. I apologize for my voice."

"We are your servants, princess. No apologies necessary, but thank you."

Kendrick smiled and looked into her eyes. Her sagging eyelids, thin red lines, and dark circles were only hidden for a moment as her shaking hands rubbed them.

"How are you, princess?"

"Kendrick, I am Althea, not princess when we are together." She pointed to the black bruise on his forehead. "Where did you get that bruise?"

A smile let him know of their connection. Kendrick gestured toward the rock. "After you."

He removed Althea's shoes. She dangled her feet in the water, and he joined her a moment later.

"This is such a pleasant haven for me. I do not know what I would do without it—or without you. From the southeastern tower window, I saw you at the market. You were watching my brother Quentin walk to the cathedral."

"The young boy with the birthmark on his left ear is your brother?"

"Yes."

"You look tired. Can I do something to help?"

"Maybe later. Now I need to talk to someone I trust."

Kendrick leaned forward and supported himself on the flat rock's edge. Althea copied his posture. When she placed her hands to support herself, her left hand landed on Kendrick's right. He instantly spread his fingers. She placed a finger in each opening.

His heart beat a little faster. A nervous energy rippled up his spine.

"Kendrick, I need you to listen then give me advice. I think I am in danger. Apparently, the archbishop is plotting my death. With my death, my brother would be king. But he is so young and impressionable. The manipulating archbishop is where my brother spends most of his time. Can you imagine my brother as king?" She took a deep breath then gazed across the stream. "Additionally, the archbishop has started rumors of invaders from the north—I think to undermine Father's authority—perhaps to block my coronation by making me out as unfit to lead a nation into battle, or perhaps to create unrest in the kingdom."

"Why are you not seeking protection from the sergeant?"

"He is the source of this information. Actually, this is his idea. We staged an argument so I would have reason to banish him to his 'observation' post after he became concerned a death threat might be looming. We determined that during the day I am never to be alone. I am either caring for Father or studying our country's affairs or preparing for the coronation ceremonies."

He lost focus on their conversation momentarily as Althea's grip tightened on his right hand. "Is your father that ill?"

"Uncertain. His current plan has him resigning his position so he can focus on the schemes against us. What should I do?"

"Cannot some of the Long Bows be assigned to protect you at night?"

"Oscar is reassigning the few trusted knights, which will take some time. Beyond them, we do not know who we can fully trust of the one hundred and fifty Long Bows. Their barracks were in the cathedral's basement for years, and several were recommended by the archbishop."

"What does the sergeant have to report?"

"I cannot be seen with him. It might jeopardize his value as a spy. If he senses danger, he will return immediately to my side."

"Perhaps I could talk to him."

Kendrick noticed a slight change in her posture and tone. "That might work. Only these four Long Bows, the sergeant, you, and I know of us. You can inform me next week."

"Also, my father. And maybe one other," he added.

"I think it's important for your father to be protecting the king, for now." She touched his right arm, and then the left side of her forehead. "Now, where did you get that bruise?"

"I ran into the ruffians from the big oak. They were seeking revenge. One hit me with a rock."

"What happened to the ruffians?"

"I am certain they will not be bothering anyone in Manshire Province."

She pointed to the sack at Kendrick's side. "I am curious, what is in the sack?"

"I have a gift for the king. My mother used to prepare it when I had breathing difficulties growing up. I hope it works for him."

"A gift for the king? What breathing difficulties?"

"It came upon me every spring until I was about twelve. In the summertime, it left, only to return the next spring." He paused and looked into her eyes. "I wish I could do something helpful, or take your struggles away," he added.

His heart beat a little faster as he pulled the two red flat stones from his pocket and handed one to Althea. "I noticed them at our last meeting and gathered them this morning. Like us, together they battle the forces working against them. You can rub it when troubled and know in your heart that I want to help you with all of mine."

He wanted so much to ask her about their future but did not want to add to her troubles or give her concern about his confidence.

"You are doing what I need. Thank you."

Haunting Blue Eyes

What once was an annual father and son project had become one of Kendrick's single responsibilities. He loaded the cart with leftover hay to trade for Reginald's extra potatoes and yams.

He was anticipating another lively conversation like he'd experienced with Reginald the past two springs. At first, Kendrick thought Reginald might have been talkative because he himself was Oscar's son, but a good friendship had developed between them.

"Reginald, how are you?"

"Doing well."

"How are your girls?"

"We are also doing well," answered Elsa, coming to the door.

"Anything exciting happen since my last visit?"

Before Reginald could stop her, Erma said, "The archbishop was here talking to Father and Mother."

"The archbishop. That's special," Kendrick said to Erma. He then turned to Reginald and raised his eyebrows, "The archbishop?" Kendrick thought *what could they possibly have in common, except maybe a prayer?*

"Girls, go help your mother while Kendrick and I unload this hay."

"Yes, Father," they said in unison.

"Thank you for the hay," Reginald said. He led Kendrick to the barn. "About the archbishop. Samantha and I are sworn to secrecy. I am struggling as I want to tell you, but I do not know what to do."

As they neared the barn it was easy to see the upgrades. Their farm, in general, was in very good condition with fresh paint on the barn doors and new fencing around the garden. Reginald always had good work clothes—like the nice light blue cotton pants and matching shirt he wore now. Kendrick and Father could not afford such maintenance expenses. And they had more land, a better harvest, and Father's Long Bow salary in comparison to Reginald's harvest income only.

"Let me make this easier for you," Kendrick began. "I will tell you something secret in exchange for your information which I believe may be important to my secret."

"I can trust you?"

"I will begin, then you can decide..." Kendrick took a deep breath. "I have been secretly meeting with the future queen. Recently, she told me her life might be in danger. She thinks the archbishop is planning to assassinate her."

"Oh my...oh my." Reginald's hand flew to his mouth. He paced inside the barn. "Oh my, it is probably true. Have a seat on the milking stool. This may take awhile."

Kendrick sat, but he wasn't comfortable. Reginald was silent, and it seemed for a time that he'd been sleepwalking.

"So what do you have to tell me?" Kendrick finally asked.

"You'll hardly believe this." The man continued to pace. "We made a deal to give up our child to be the king's heir." He paused, and looked out the door, then paced faster. His hands were in constant unrest—in his pockets, on his hips, crossed in front of him or behind his neck. Reginald appeared uncomfortable.

"The strange thing about the adoption is we traded for this farm, the same farm in which we could have grown food to feed the baby." Kendrick turned his gaze to the floor and smiled at the irony.

"A few weeks after the birth, we returned to our ransacked house and barn. Every container had been opened. Someone even went through the weeds piled on the other side of the barn. We spent three days putting everything back."

"What were they looking for?"

Reginald stopped pacing and placed his hands on the top of his head as he looked toward the dirt floor. Reginald still appeared bothered, but he continued:

"We had guards watching us for eight months in Saraton. And Oscar came quarterly to check on us."

"My father was involved?" His voice was shaky and soft.

"Yes. He arranged the deal between the king and us. In fact, for our protection, he suggested we get a letter from the king describing the agreement."

For Kendrick, the initial shock of his father's involvement wore off quickly, for he had always assumed some of his father's work was secret.

"Who ransacked the house?"

"Not sure, but I suspect they were looking for the king's letter. Or, maybe anything that might connect us to the princess or king. We have kept our part of the deal. Two weeks ago, the archbishop came to our home and asked many questions. We were confused by some of them. He knows our daughter is the princess."

"How did he suspect you were involved?"

"He saw Samantha's bright blue eyes at the Easter service. Their likeness to the princess's blue eyes was unmistakable. Then there were the mysterious disappearances of the captain of the Long Bows—who returned on the day of the princess's birth."

ANDEAN WHITE

Balconies and Draw Bridges

Princess Althea stood by the king's desk. She'd had enough of the visitors' chairs and her father looking down on her.

"You are sure this will work?" King Louis III asked.

"I have got to reach him with something that I think will interest him," Althea replied. "We have such a poor relationship, I am guessing that this will work. If he does not show, we will know."

"Are you in any danger?"

"Only if he decides to kill me before the invaders."

They had spent many hours together. When he'd crossed his arms, Althea knew his concern had changed to resolution.

The week previous, after a chance meeting, he'd suggested an attempt at a private meeting with Quentin. They'd met where the stairway from the chambers and first floor exit converged.

"Quentin was alone walking to class at the cathedral library. He told me he was studying mathematics and mythology. Zeus the leader, Thor the trusted soldier, and Calypso the secret keeper are his favorite characters. He talked about their characteristics and how they reminded him of me as the king, Oscar as the soldier, and he as the secret keeper. He was quick to answer my questions, and he had a tone of superiority. I am concerned that Bettina might be one of Archbishop Thomas's spies."

After a moment of silence while the king stroked his beard, he said, "Humor me with a review of this plan."

"I will have the sergeant start a rumor that the invaders plan to kill us tomorrow night—you in your chambers and me in the courtyard. The courtyard can be watched from only two locations. I will be waiting at the north balcony, which is the most convenient to his room. The sergeant can signal me if he goes to the south alcove."

"This sounds like something I would think up. Have the sergeant ready in the event something goes wrong." Father paused momentarily and raised his right eyebrow. A sly smile appeared. He continued, "And Bettina?"

"The assistant chef has invited her to the kitchen to make pastries." She considered telling Father that Bettina liked the assistant chef and had asked for the baking lesson as a way to spend time with him. And so she'd arranged the cooking class, though she'd decided she would reveal the truth of the matter later, after she'd confirmed the sergeant's suspicion about the assistant cook.

The king raised an eyebrow and tilted his head.

"It's coincidental," she continued. "But fortunate. That's why we need to act while she is busy."

"Althea, be very careful."

"Yes, Father." She did not want to remind him there were actually four locations where an assassin could hide if they decided to kill her.

As she closed the door her heart beat faster. Her brother, Quentin, was an impressionable eleven-year old boy, which could work both against her and for her. Careful wording was a priority to send him the right message because Quentin was an unknown factor; Bettina had always been with Quentin.

Walking across the courtyard she ran both hands through her hair. If anyone were a witness, they'd think she was worried about something. But for the sergeant, it signaled approval to start rumors.

* * *Oscar* * *

"Oscar, Althea is going to attempt a meeting with Quentin tomorrow evening without Bettina," the king said.

"Do you want me to protect her?"

"Yes. The sergeant might be occupied protecting her from a disadvantaged location. And to get him in an ideal position leaves Althea vulnerable for three to four minutes."

"You are suspecting that Quentin will tell Bettina?"

"Not sure. Althea heard Quentin and Bettina arguing last night. Their relationship might be unstable. But if Thomas finds out, he might take the opportunity to cover his actions within the invader's lie."

* * *Althea* * *

The night air was cool, pleasant actually. She closed her eyes hoping to calm her nerves. Mentally, she rehearsed her opening lines and wondered what actors did before the play began. The faint sound of footsteps caught her attention. Slightly turning her head improved her hearing.

Althea was surprised by how much he had grown beyond his years. He looked like Mother, but tall like Father. His walk was confident and his head held high. The thought of this meeting's irony produced a half smile. *How can we live in the same castle and see so little of each other?*

Father had cautioned her to be patient and let time increase the anxiety of this clandestine situation. It would give Althea an advantage. Father had said her absence from the courtyard would make Quentin antsy, and would begin to worry him about getting caught.

The prince positioned himself in a dark area of the north balcony and watched the courtyard. Althea walked from the shadows.

"Sorry to disappoint you," she said.

The prince flinched and turned toward the voice. "You scared me! What are you doing here?" His eyes looked from one location to another.

"Quentin, it is just you and I." She held her palms open to indicate she was alone. "I would like to talk without Bettina answering the questions, or keeping us apart. You are free to go if you wish. But you will always wonder what could have been."

"Go ahead," Quentin replied. "And just so you know, Bettina does not always speak for me." Quentin looked away.

"First, Father sends his love."

"Humph!"

"It is true."

"Then why does he never have birthday parties for me? You have one every year." He paced.

"Bettina says you are shy and would be uncomfortable with so many kids."

"It is because the king doesn't like me. He thinks I am slow witted and would embarrass him. Bettina told me—several times. You are trying to confuse me."

* * *Oscar* * *

Oscar admired Althea's courage, but thought she should not be in this dangerous situation. He continued to scan the locations where an archer could hide with a view of the balcony. One floor below, next to the village guard tower and across from the balcony, the sergeant scanned the shadows.

Now a dark figure revealed itself on the roof in the shadow of the village guard tower, just above the sergeant. The figure moved with the craftiness of a fox.

Oscar scrutinized the area. There was nothing soft to set an arrow in to get the sergeant's attention. He crawled backwards from his lookout position to the peak of the roof then slipped behind the roofline, moving quickly below it toward the guard tower. Occasionally, he peered over the edge to see if the shadow remained. Making his way to the other side of the roof next to the guard tower, he climbed the incline, and just as suddenly slipped. The noise was enough to announce his position. He gathered himself and rushed to the roof's peak. The shadow was gone.

* * *Althea* * *

"Take a few days to think about this conversation," Althea said. "Also, think about why the archbishop is plotting against the monarchy, and what he gains if *you* are the king."

"There has always been a king—never a queen," Quentin replied.

"Father's health is dictating that the older heir rule the country. You will still be too young if Father lives another two years." She paused. *She would also be too young*.

Quentin blinked at her. In his eyes Althea saw doubt.

"Tell me about Mother."

From his wide-eyed stare, she assumed he was asking about Father's distant emotions as it related to his looks. She considered asking for clarity, but decided the answer she wanted him to receive was best served by answering his question.

"You would have loved her. She was a wonderful mother. Loving. Always teaching."

"It's so unfair. You have had everything. I have had nothing. Mother tucked you in at night, she read to you, and took you to the market." He blinked once more, turned, and unexpectedly left the balcony. The torch in the hall lit his silhouette as he retreated. And just as she had done, he was running his hands through his hair.

* * *

King Louis III knocked on the door.

"Come in, Father."

"Well?"

"It is as we suspected. He came to see an assassination, mine. He is bitter. In his mind, I have had everything—he has had nothing. Much of his replies start or end with 'Bettina said...'."

"Hmmm."

It was time to ask. Another opportunity like this may never happen again. "Father...*why* was Quentin *abandoned*?"

Father turned away. "He looks like your mother." He paused. "I see her in him, and I cannot take losing her again." He pressed his palms against his forehead. "I do not want him punished because of me."

"Who would punish him?"

"Nature, the gods, the cosmos...I am not sure and I am not taking a chance. Four of my sons have already died."

She brushed her hair. The long, blond strands fell in front of her shoulder. *Father had always been superstitious.*

"You know you alienated him. And his only influence is Bettina, whom we now suspect is part of the archbishop's spy network," Althea said. "You taught me to scrutinize every detail of a scheme. How could you be so negligent?"

"Bettina is more than a suspect, daughter. While Bettina was having cooking lessons, I searched her room. I found a bloody monogrammed handkerchief hidden in her clothes—the initials were TIS, Thomas Ignacio Smythe.

There is also a hunting knife with *Family* carved in the scabbard." The king took a deep breath. "Bettina has fooled me for a little more than twelve years," he continued. "She was a good spy."

"We could have avoided most of this plotting and counter-plotting if you had evaluated the details." Her voice had a stinging tone.

The king glanced toward Althea. "I trusted her with Quentin. Her version of Quentin remained consistent through the years. My fear of cursing him was a great mistake. I see that now." He paced for a few moments. "Maybe he is not too old to save? Did you get a sense that he was conflicted? Will we be able to unravel their handiwork? And do you think we can undo all the lies they have fed him?"

* * *Quentin* * *

The mind was a powerful force.

Youth was a powerful gift.

Revenge was a powerful act.

Disrupted sleep continued throughout the night, followed by an early rise. Both were uncommon events for Quentin. He went down the spiral staircase at the rear of the castle. Throughout the day, his aimless meandering took him by unpleasant locations. At the back of the butcher shop he was shocked back to reality by the stench of the meat scraps. The clanking of the hammer making horseshoes kept a steady pace in his memory for nearly half an hour. He nearly fell into the pit where the kitchen buckets were dumped. He tripped into a pile of decaying weeds and various stable refuse.

Quentin wanted resolution. He couldn't go to Bettina, or could he? Was she really an evil villainess? Or did his sister just want to trick him? She'd probably lied to the archbishop also.

Maybe he could approach the archbishop—he had always been kind to him. Or, maybe he could talk to the sergeant. He too had been cast out. He had been confined to that stool by the gate by Althea after their big argument. They were kindred souls, so to speak; both had lost favor with the monarchy.

The archbishop had spies in the Long Bows—if only he knew who they were.

Quentin rubbed his head. He looked to his right then to his left and behind. He could see no one. He crouched and moved behind the drawbridge mechanism.

"Who goes there?" the sergeant inquired. He did not move and continued to whittle.

"Quentin."

"Quentin, the king's son?"

"Yes...well, maybe..."

"How can I help you?"

"You were assigned to protect Althea. Is she an honest person? Would she lie to me?"

There was a short laugh, almost two small to hear. But Quentin had heard it. "Your sister is stubborn and opinionated, but she is not a liar. She speaks the truth regardless of the pain it might bring."

Quentin tried to dust the stains off his knees, though some of it remained. He wandered inside the side wagon gate and crossed to the cathedral. Placing his hand on the door handle, he waited, troubling thoughts continuing within his mind. He removed his hand. *Who could he trust? Why was he hesitating? The archbishop had treated him well. He had to trust someone.* He opened the cathedral door with a temporary confidence.

Looking up at the ceiling, his eyes rested on his favorite panel. It was Christ rising from the dead, just as he, himself would one day rise to the throne.

The whole thing fascinated him. The building itself was taller than the trees, though it did not bend in the wind. It was quieter than the forest and filled with inspirational paintings and windows. In reality it was the only place he felt safe, and important.

The archbishop silently stepped to Quentin's side.

"Good afternoon, Quentin. I was not sure you would show. You are quite late today. Are you ready for your weekly study time?"

"No, I have been pondering my station in life. Bettina may have been lying to the king and to you. She *has* been lying to me."

"Why do you say that?" He pointed to the pew to sit.

"Bettina has told the king more than once that I am slow witted and that is why he does not give me birthday parties or spend time with me. He is embarrassed to be seen with me. She apparently told him I was not good with people and would cower in the corner."

Archbishop Thomas drummed his fingers. "I thought this might happen. She has become possessive and wants to keep you to herself. I will speak to her tomorrow. This is a common care taker problem that I can fix."

"What do you know about my sister, Althea?"

"Same as you. She will be the queen upon the king's death. She is being trained for this task, unless..." The archbishop stopped speaking and waited for Quentin to make eye contact. "I need you to swear the secret I am about to tell you will not be repeated to anyone."

"Yes, I swear. What secret?"

The archbishop drummed his fingers again. "Historically, the leader of Manshire Province has been the eldest male of the Harden family. For the first time this may not be true. The Manshire law requires the next ruler to be the eldest heir over thirteen years of age. Until now it was always assumed the heir would be the oldest male. The law is not specific. But King Louis III has taken another liberty, which we are certain will not be acceptable to the province." He stared at a spot on the floor.

Quentin wondered if he was being manipulated. Was he not to be included in the planning of his own future? The archbishop had a plan, which included him, still he hadn't confided in him until he'd asked.

"Quentin, I am about to tell you the treasure of all secrets which you must keep to yourself. It's very important that we use this information at the right time to ensure the safe transfer of power to you. Can you keep this confidential?"

Quentin's interest was stimulated, but his patience was being challenged. He was about to hear the path to the throne that Bettina had told him he was born for. "Yes. I swear I am prepared to keep this secret."

"Althea is adopted from a mother and father not related to the king or queen."

The archbishop was quiet for a few moments, and Quentin thought about all of his ambitions and preparations to become king.

"Queen Francine, your mother, had trouble giving birth; all of her previous children had died at birth or near birth. You are the only true and living heir."

Until now the pieces of the puzzle had merely floated about in his mind, but now...Quentin could see the pieces fitting together.

"This is fantastic. The Knight Games are next week. We can announce this information at the games. Maybe I can ask the king to let me sit at the podium so I can be close to see his reaction!"

"You are just twelve, and eleven months from thirteen. We must have a little patience. The king's health will probably force him to resign in the next few months. Althea will become the new queen. We will keep her busy with rumors of foreign threats, and a return of the birthing plague from a few years ago." A slight smile appeared on the archbishop's relaxed face.

"If we wait until the king dies, we will not have to contend with his interference," the archbishop continued.

"He is quite ill. Finally, we will reveal she is not of the king's lineage, and that you are the rightful heir."

"Are you sure I will be king?" he asked. *It would be a fine thing to do whatever he wanted to do; to no longer be ordered about by Bettina.*

"My sources tell me he is digressing rapidly—maybe three to five months," Archbishop Thomas said. He paused again to stare at the floor, and the stress returned to his face.

"How long have you known about the adoption?" Quentin asked.

"A couple of months. Remember you must keep this quiet so the king does not change the laws or something more drastic."

* * *Bettina* * *

Bettina checked the bell tower window. The red sash had been removed, telling her that a new development in the plan had just recently come to pass. She hoped it didn't mean another delay. Still, like Uncle Thomas, she enjoyed the warm August nights. The dawn meetings interfered with her best sleep.

As she approached the meeting location, Thomas napped on the warm boulder while he waited. Hunter, the assistant cook, was sitting against a nearby stone.

"Good, we are all here."

"I wanted to advise you of a change of plans. I have changed our target date to takeover this monarchy until after the king dies. We will have an easier path with only the princess to dethrone, or assassinate."

"This is the second time we have delayed our plans," Hunter said.

"It's only the second time for you," Bettina said to Hunter. She turned to the archbishop.

"You've postponed the plans several times lately. Is this a delay tactic? Are you afraid?" she asked.

"I am certain after yesterday that Quentin is not quite ready," the archbishop returned. "But we can solve the problem within a couple of months."

"Yesterday?" Bettina asked. "I looked for him all day."

"Quentin stopped by to talk to me, apparently after walking around questioning his life's purpose. Hunter, you will inform our two Long Bows?"

"Yes, your grace."

Archbishop Thomas looked into each of their eyes and found frustration. "What is wrong?"

"It is the delay. I am afraid we will be caught and hung for treason," Hunter said.

"It is time to extract our revenge," Bettina offered.

"If the king is still alive in ninety days, we will execute the plan. Agreed?"

"Agreed."

"We will meet after the king dies to adjust our plans. I will leave first—I want to enjoy these wonderful warm mornings while they last."

Night Before Knights

Kendrick's night was filled with fitful sleep—and strange dreams. Worrying about Althea and Father only made matters worse. Tonight the same nightmare took away his dreams.

> *Draco, the Dragon of the night sky, carried a dark angel, whose silhouette blocked the stars as she passed above.*
>
> *Kendrick could not see the whip but could hear it strike Draco.*
>
> *On Pegasus, Kendrick could not direct him quick enough to respond to Draco's wild flight.*
>
> *Every pass above the castle another of Kendrick's friends or family became a target of the diamond-shaped scepter as it sent flames toward them, though Kendrick had managed to block most of the flames with the family shield.*
>
> *The dark angel's scepter gave life to Draco.*
>
> *After several passes Pegasus had exhausted his energy...*

An exhausted Kendrick woke feeling sweaty and helpless. Being informed of the conspiracies had made him feel important but still an outsider. The ambush followed by the convalescing and contemplation had made him worry his skills were not adequate to protect Althea and the king, and perhaps his father.

He paced until his father's voice broke his thoughts.

"Son, try to get some rest. The games are friendly."

"I am worried something big is in the near future— as early as tomorrow or possibly after the games."

"Kendrick, rely on your instincts tomorrow. Unusual behavior, knights talking and eerily looking at observers, covert handling of small concealed weapons, notes being passed, that kind of thing. This is the last public event for months. If the archbishop is planning an assassination, he needs to justify his actions to the kingdom, to make the transition to Quentin stick. This is a golden opportunity for his cause—the people on his revenge list will be there, he will have an audience, and few will challenge him in public. And King Louis will know the archbishop has achieved his promised revenge."

"All this started by a boyhood prank?"

"It's not just the prank, it is his lost dignity. We've exposed his weakness. It is the embarrassment and shame he feels, the loss of two playmates, and the options that we took from him. Consider the single, lonely jobs he's had where he would never feel powerless and vulnerable again. Consider the strained relationship between the king and the archbishop; two stubborn—no three with me."

"You have thought a lot about this."

"It's been worry every day. Can you sleep now?"

"I will try."

Kendrick finally slept. He dreamed that the dark angel slapped him with the diamond scepter and tried to burn him.

* * *Quentin* * *

"Where have you been?" Bettina asked as Quentin entered her adjoining room.

"Getting something to eat. Why do you care?"

"I need to know where you are at all times. The archbishop has asked me to take care of you."

Maybe it was the newly revealed lies. Maybe it was the frustration of being alone trying to sort out the confusion. Or maybe it was his growing hormones. But, Quentin was angry. "*He is not my father! He is just the bishop.*"

She slapped him.

"Do not talk about my uncle like that. He is the archbishop! You would be dead if it weren't for him."

"Like my four previous brothers?" He rubbed his cheek.

"I will be happy to be rid of you. You are rude, egotistical, self-centered, and naïve. My uncle should have picked a different boy." She turned away from him.

"You have had a good life caring for me—warm place, good food, and nice clothes."

Her voice grew louder. "I had a good life until your father invaded Saraton. He turned my father into a soldier and placed my family in peril so the king could have *more hunting land.*"

"My father does not even hunt!" He wasn't sure if this was true or not, but he had to take his frustration out on Bettina, the liar. "It is a lie like the others from you. Like the lies *you* told my father—that I am slow-witted, afraid of people, not smart enough to be king."

"Oh!" Bettina fumbled. There was no heated response back, and in moments had left the room.

Quentin blinked. What had just happened? He heard the drawer slide and hit the floor. Bettina returned a few seconds later. She pulled a knife from a scabbard that said *Family*. "I may not *wait* to kill you," she said.

Quentin turned, opened the door, and slammed it behind him. At that moment, something plunged into the heavy wood.

He ran! But where could he go? It had to be somewhere that Bettina would never look for or enter. He considered the stables, the cathedral or the kitchen, but they were all too obvious. The Long Bow's barracks! That would be the safest place.

Not part of the original building, the barracks had been added next to the inside of the outer curtain so the knights could rush to their posts in an emergency. The stones were much smaller than those of the castle and the area above the roof was storage.

Quentin approached the guard. "May I stay here tonight? My tutor snores loudly and I want to be alert tomorrow."

"Yes, young Prince. Use the bottom bunk third on the right. It's mine."

Quentin opened the thick door and stepped into the barracks. There were four rows of bunk beds with various sized wooden footlockers. Each bed had the same dull brown wool bedding. The guard's bed was wrinkle free. Quentin was careful to be quiet. He lay on his back on top of the made bed staring at the underside of the bunk above.

Tea Time

* * *Bettina* * *

"Come in," called the archbishop through the door. "Ah, Bettina so nice to see you." Thomas sat on his bed with his back to the headboard. He laid the journal on the bed.

"I have come to apologize for my behavior at Camel Humps," Bettina started. "You have been good to me, kept me fed, clothed, and warm. I get so angry at the suffering you and I have endured by the king."

"It will be over soon. Then we can reclaim the Smythe family's natural place."

"What are you reading?"

"The former priest's journal. It is really quite interesting. Would you like me to read it to you?"

"Before you start is there some tea?"

"Yes, in the pitcher on the table. The librarian brought it about ten minutes ago."

She spooned the loose leaves in a strainer and poured the water for two teas. "Please read on, uncle." She watched him reach for the journal then dipped the strainer once in her cup. As she carried the cup to Thomas she bounced the strainer to strengthen the tea. What a peaceful setting.

He sipped the tea and set it aside. "It is a little warm."

"Yes, I am waiting for it to cool some." She sat next to him on the bed.

"August 13. It is Friday the thirteenth. The staff skipped the Friday swim at the pond—it could be difficult next week. The cathedral cat, Midnight, was jumpy by the end of the day. No one would pet her and everyone walked away. I wonder what the cat ..."

Uncle Thomas was silent. His eyelids slowly closed and the journal fell forward onto his chest. She walked to the head of the bed. The color had already begun to disappear from his face. She checked his wrists for a pulse.

A sudden knock at the door made her jump.

"Is everything all right?" asked the librarian. She opened the door and handed the man a bag of gold coins. "Thank you. You best move to another town."

The hinges creaked as the door swung slowly to close. When the door met the frame, the clunk signaled her to slide the latch.

From the armoire she selected the same vestments as he'd worn on Easter. At the writing table, she checked to see if there was stationary. The vestments were draped over a chair back while she collected the journal. Scanning the journal she looked for the end of the sentence that Uncle Thomas hadn't finished—"must think us as superstitious humans." She placed the book on the writing table then began to dress the dead archbishop over his nightclothes.

"Uncle, you have become afraid of the king. This is why you need me to implement your revenge. You will not have to tell us there is another delay. We cannot wait to take our rightful place alongside the king and princess. The invaders will be blamed for this death..."

She lifted the archbishop's feet and slid the white linen, tunic like, alb over his legs. She rocked the man from side to side and pulled the alb so she could fasten the girdle at his waist. She covered his bare feet with shoes.

"You will be eulogized with the king and princess— and, maybe the Prince. I will decide tomorrow. I am more than happy to expedite your well planned rise to power. By the way, I still think we need more help."

Lifting his torso she placed the blue silk outer chasuble over his head and slid it under his body. She tugged on the hem to straighten the robe.

"The librarian was easy to bribe. "Skinny" took some negotiating, but he fell prey to gold. Did you know he was a former Saraton Special Guard? A mercenary, so to speak, the strangest things you find out about people. You wonder where I got the money?"

She struggled to lift the lifeless body and dress him.

"It's from the sale of the family business you left me. Oh, you did not get to use any of the money? You should not have made yourself so valuable by leaving your portion to me upon your death."

The gold cope was placed over his head, and smoothed out over his shoulders. Gently he was laid on the bed. She folded his arms over his stomach.

"The king and his associates will be surprised at the variety of delivery of death. The king will be the last to go. He has to witness the full revenge of the Smythe family. Can I use your stationary? Thank you. I need to leave a letter, I think.

She hand-pressed the wrinkles on the gold cope.

"Uncle Thomas why did you *sell* me to the queen? But perhaps you wanted me to become the caregiver, a commoner, so you could achieve your plan...but Quentin... Hunter did not prepare *the* tea for the queen when she was pregnant with Quentin. Oh! You were surprised by the birth of Althea. I think you thought the tea had failed. But the king had a backup plan. That's funny!"

"Your big mistake? Not taking action after Grandfather, Grandmother, Mother, and Father drowned. That is where I started to think you did not have it in you to work your plan. Yes, I'd planned to steal the case of tea you ordered, but the wind blew it away. Could have been funny, but it wasn't. By the time I found the case, most of it had been stolen. As you can see, I did manage to get enough for your special brew, however.

"So, did you ever wonder what your life would have been like if you'd taken over the family business? Oh well! Really big excitement planned for the Knight Games. You can read the letter if you want but please put it back in the envelope."

She placed the archbishop's hat on his head and wrote the letter, which was afterwards placed under his folded hands. Bettina straightened the writing table and checked the archbishop's clothing.

Leaving him there, she took the back stairwell and entered the library behind the counter. The librarian was waiting in a chair by the door.

She was surprised. "What are you still doing here?" she asked.

"If I run, they will think I killed the archbishop. If I leave in a few days, people will think I moved onto another job," the librarian replied.

"Smart. Thank you for your help. Enjoy the money."

"Thank you. You saved me from having to kill him myself," the librarian offered, laughing.

Her curiosity was piqued. "I saved *you*?"

"Yes. I am Howard Rochester, the son of Gilford Rochester. Probably doesn't mean much to you, but your grandfather stole silver coins from Rochester & Son. Then, he used those coins to bribe the port master. That put us out of business. You are the last living Smythe heir. I like you and enjoyed our time together. Enjoy your new wealth. It was nice to meet you, Bettina."

She fingered the knife in the bag with her left hand but decided to leave it there.

"Thank you for being a good friend. By the way, how did you know about my new wealth?"

"I listened at the door."

Revenge Requires Re-planning

Awakened by the activity of Long Bows preparing for the Knight Games, Quentin leaned on his elbows.

"How are you this morning?" the sergeant asked.

"Better. Thank you for letting me sleep here."

"So your tutor snores?" The sergeant squeezed between the bunks, placed his hand on Quentin's shoulder, then sat on the adjacent bunk.

"What? ...Oh, yes. Really bad some times."

"Can I help you with anything?"

"No, I am...all right. Well...maybe. I need some advice and a bath."

"Let us take care of the bath first. Come with me. You can use our bath. I will gather some fresh clothes for you."

The sergeant returned with fresh undergarments, socks, pants, and a shirt. Quentin dried himself with a towel.

"Follow me to the captain's quarters. As you trust me, you can trust him."

"Welcome to the Long Bows, Prince Quentin. The sergeant says you want some advice," Oscar said. "Sit." He pointed to the chair.

"I have a dilemma for which I cannot find a conclusion. I have a father who is not a friend, and a friend who is a father. My father, whom I rarely speak to, sends his love by messenger. My friend is my father's enemy, but he is cordial and helpful to me," Quentin said. "But his niece is crazy..."

Oscar frowned, but inside something else was churning...

"I, too, have an uncommon relationship with my son, Kendrick, but it is grounded in love. I am away for long periods of time; he is left to fend for himself. He had a difficult time when he was your age. He wanted my attention and approval—approval that I was not available to give him. But he learned to make decisions on his own. Regarding your father, he has kept this distance because he is afraid he is cursed. And he doesn't want the curse to hurt you."

"Do I have an adopted sister?" Quentin asked.

Oscar and the sergeant exchanged looks—the sergeant's was one of disbelief, and Oscar couldn't believe the boy knew. Which meant the archbishop knew! What could he do? Perhaps only one thing: show the boy that he was his top priority.

"We will get back to your last question in a while. First, let us discuss your other concern," Oscar began. "I am a big believer that fate is our destiny. And, how we respond to its challenges determines our happiness. If we resist fate, we can be very unhappy, and it will alter our course, making our life more difficult. If we go with fate, we can enjoy a good life."

"How has your life been?"

"A bit of both. I have gone with fate and have been happy. I have resisted fate and have been very sad."

Quentin looked thoughtfully to the floor. Oscar motioned to the sergeant and whispered, "Tell the king to wait for me before entering the arena. And sergeant, do not speak of the adoption."

Quentin looked up at the sergeant as he left them. "There are two plans to put me on the throne," he began.

"One begins today. Unfortunately, I do not know which one is active."

"Tell me," Oscar prodded, his heart thundering in his chest.

"The archbishop's preferred plan is waiting for the king to die from his disease. Let Althea take the throne, and either by assassination, uprising, or revealing she is adopted..." He looked up at Oscar for seeming confirmation, "then remove her from the throne when I reach thirteen."

Quentin stood, placed his hands on his hips, and began to pace the room. "I am not sure of the details of Bettina's *preferred* plan. But I think it calls for Althea to be assassinated publicly at the games and her adoption made public at the same time. You are to be ambushed by three knights within a few days possibly as soon as today. Kendrick's death is also planned for today—at the games. Father is to be poisoned in three months if the disease does not take him first."

"How do you know this?"

"I was meeting with the archbishop yesterday. He told me about the king's secret, his options for dealing with Althea, and how he planned to implement their plan. The other plan I overheard, Bettina talking with someone she called Skinny. This was after she threw a knife at me."

He was impressed with Quentin's education. For a twelve year old, the prince was very mature, and certainly smarter than Oscar had been led to believe.

* * *Quentin* * *

Quentin waited outside the door a few moments and thought about the times he had peeked through the door latch to listen in on her and Father. He knocked.

"Enter."

"Good morning, sister."

"Good morning—brother." A quick smile appeared on her face.

Althea lay her brush on the table and turned her chair toward Quentin. She motioned for him to sit on the edge of the bed.

"I have thought about our meeting on the balcony. The archbishop has a plan to gain control of the throne that requires me to be king. His *only* interest in me is access to the throne. And I think Bettina is his partner. I've heard parts of conversations between them that did not mean much until he revealed his plan. The archbishop is on a revenge quest that I think goes back to childhood." Quentin paused as he thought about the change he was about to make. Bettina's knife throwing and the realization that he was a tool being used within the archbishop selfish revenge plan left him with a hollow feeling.

He continued, "I wish to tell you a secret that I think you deserve to know and that the archbishop has plans to use."

Althea leaned forward and placed her hands on her knees.

"I do not know how to say this politely. The archbishop has evidence you are adopted by the king. Your real parents are a farmer and his wife."

There was a moment of silence much longer than Quentin had anticipated. Althea stared at him. A tear developed inside her eye. He watched it slide down her cheek before she decided to wipe it.

"They lied to us to justify their objectives," Quentin said. "Our respective father figures are using us both. Our father, the king, switched you for a still birth baby to be his heir to the throne. Our father, the archbishop, plans to manipulate me to control the kingdom and fulfill his revenge and greed. I assume, after my usefulness is over, I will be removed from the throne after the laws have been changed, allowing the archbishop to be king."

"Are you sure of this information?"

"The archbishop has had several plans to remove you from office, all of which are designed to bring the king, and you, great embarrassment—then death!"

A single note from a trumpet signaled the beginning of the Knight Games.

"We have to go. We are in the opening procession." She put her arm around Quentin. "Thank you."

Knight Games

The calm air contained a suggestion of autumn. The soft wood leaves of light green would soon transition to yellow, gold, orange, red, and brown. The cuffs of the white plastered walls supporting the seating area were darkened from the mud carried into the arena. The weathered oak seating planks bowed between the supports when occupied. Each side of the octagon shaped arena contained twenty rows of seats, except for the monarchy's section. The arena dirt floor was large enough for horse racing.

Spectators buzzed like bees looking for prime seats and covering spaces, laying down family quilts for those yet to come. A father and son competition brought additional excitement to these games. The fact that the father was the captain of the Long Bows and the son, a guardian of the market, raised the interest.

The king's scout waited on the podium for the arena to settle down and fill. He exited the arena and signaled the trumpet. The three violins, French horn, trumpet, and a single snare drum played the nation's anthem while the king, Althea, and Quentin entered at ground level.

The five seats reserved for the archbishop and cathedral staff were empty.

As the participants bowed, the royalty ascended the stairs to their seats. The king's nod appeared to start the games, but his eyes were directed to Oscar, who glanced at the empty cathedral staff seats, then responded with a nod.

The participants walked to the staging and preparation area under the stands. A line of support posts divided the area into three spaces. Although sunlight leaked between the seat sections and thousands of small spots, it was quite dark. After his eyes adjusted, Oscar could see where previous contestants had carved their initials into the support posts.

The first event had two components—distance running and short consecutive sprints. Half the field of fifty ran the distance course while the others completed the sprints. The running event came easy to Kendrick—he was younger than the other participants and did not own a horse. At the end of round one the top scores belonged to Hunter, Kendrick, sergeant, one of the Long Bows, and Oscar. He suppressed a smile when he heard the crowd cheering.

The set-up of the knife throwing took about an hour and required the participants to help. A juggling team, two men and a lady, kept the audience entertained. The juggling clubs were tossed between the two men facing each other and back-to-back. For their finale the female juggler stood on one of the male's shoulders.

Kendrick worked at station number ten—near the podium. His efforts to catch Althea's eye went unsatisfied. Twice she placed her hands on the chair's arms to stand up, but seconds later rested in the chair. Each time the king turned to Althea, she would shoo her father away like a bug.

The king glanced at the archbishop's empty seats frequently.

Oscar worried their lack of a counter-plan put them at too great a risk, and wondered if perhaps the archbishop had altered his plans because Quentin had "changed sides." Were they vulnerable?

At the completion of the set-up, a whistle signaled the participants; it was time to begin. Oscar entered the staging area last. Before leaving the arena Oscar checked the king's signal. The king had placed his right hand on his own left shoulder—the sign that they needed to meet.

When he felt safe, Oscar slipped out of the staging area and walked to the guarded door under the royal podium. The guards nodded to Oscar before he entered what he remembered as a stale smelling corridor. After climbing the poorly lit stairs, he slowly slid the small panel open behind the king's chair.

"King Louis, I am here," Oscar whispered.

"Appear normal," said the king. "...and check on the archbishop. He should be here. I am concerned about his absence."

* * *Oscar* * *

Oscar ran to the cathedral. He entered into the main assembly hall and called for Archbishop Thomas. The librarian ran toward Oscar, waving his arms in front, scolded him with "Shhhh!", and avoided eye contact.

"Where is the archbishop?"

"He is ill."

"How do you know?"

"He will not answer my inquiry."

"Take me to his room." Oscar ran his hand along the bowstring stretched across his chest. He adjusted his quiver and took a deep breath.

"The archbishop needs his sleep to recover."

"Take me to him, or you will see the inside of our jail."

"Follow me, sir." He never looked at Oscar's eyes.

They walked, climbed stairs, and traversed hallways for several minutes. Oscar thought the librarian was taking the long way, until he said, "The archbishop's quarters."

Oscar knocked. "Thomas, are you there?"

"It is Archbishop Thomas," the librarian corrected. He continued to watch the floor.

"Archbishop Thomas, are you there?" Oscar yelled. But there was nothing. No reply. No snoring. Oscar opened the door.

The archbishop didn't move. He was in full vestments and his skin was a whitish-grey. Oscar touched his cold hand. The man was dead.

A chill, like the darkest part of winter filled his veins. Had the archbishop died of his own accord or had someone murdered him? He turned to the librarian. The man was literally shaking. Tears were filling his eyes.

"Do *not* let anyone in this room," Oscar said. "And, do *not* leave this location under any circumstances. Do! You! Understand?"

"I understand," the librarian's voice quivered.

Oscar slid the envelope from underneath the archbishop's crossed hands.

* * *

Kendrick kept watching for Oscar. Number twenty-two began to throw as Oscar covertly handed the envelope to Kendrick. "Keep this safe at all costs. I will retrieve it after I complete the knife throwing event."

Kendrick squared his shoulders and raised his chin. He knew the letter was safe.

Oscar adjusted the knife on his belt.

A large cross-section of a tree trunk was target number one. Each successive target got smaller and further from the throwing line—ten targets total. Scores were awarded based on targets hit; more points were given for difficulty and proximity to the center.

The leaders threw at the end of the event.

Kendrick stepped inside the arena to watch his father's unusual throwing action. Oscar pulled his knife from the scabbard and threw it in a single stroke at the target. The crowd gasped at the skill unmatched by the previous contestants who'd released their knives after an aiming cast. Oscar moved through the first five targets quickly.

At target number six, Oscar glanced at the princess. Her eyes were fixed on the arena dirt in front of the podium and his knife missed the target. Silence spread through the audience. Targets seven through ten were perfect scores.

Thus far Oscar had completed the event with the highest score.

He returned to the staging area to retrieve the letter.

* * *Kendrick* * *

For Kendrick, knife throwing was a challenging skill. In his mind, the sharp tip of the knife actually pointed at the target only an instant with each rotation. He managed to hit within, or near, the targets on all locations except for number eight which stuck in the wood, though not near the center.

Kendrick came in sixth for the event but remained in fourth place overall. His combined score was a few points ahead of the sergeant, who was surprisingly complementary and encouraging. His name was not announced as one of the top three leaders. He shook his head.

Set-up for the obstacle course would take over an hour, allowing participants to break for lunch. Samantha had prepared a lunch for Kendrick of chicken, bread, milk, and water.

It was extremely hard work setting up the course. Clydesdales were used to drag large logs and boulders into place. The shuffling and hooves pulling heavy logs for the next event echoed in the staging area. Kendrick

177

visualized their large hooves slamming into the earth and their powerful muscles flexing as they pulled loads weighing more than themselves. The thunder of the mighty Clydesdales fired his confidence.

The competitors in the staging area had separated into three groups. The knights out of the competition gathered along the far edge of staging receiving condolences. The competing knights gathered in the middle. There was laughing and shoulder slapping. The three civilian guests—Kendrick, Hunter, and a burly man— huddled together, quiet and wondering. Kendrick shared his lunch with them. He was also trying to figure out where he had last seen Hunter.

* * *Oscar* * *

The king, Quentin, and Oscar met at the king's chambers during the obstacle course set-up.

"We should go ahead. We can inform Althea later," the king said.

"Do you think the princess has already been killed?" Quentin asked.

"No. She was headed for the staging area as we came here. Probably going to talk to Kendrick," Oscar answered.

Now was the time.

Oscar slipped his knife through the closing fold. He removed the letter and read it aloud.

To Whom It May Concern:

Uncle Thomas has been relieved of his burden to execute his plan. The heavy weight of his revenge was carried for far too long. Seems he was waiting for the perfect moment... He can now

178

rest in peace. I am not afraid to take care of this for him.

As for the king, he has abused Uncle Thomas. It began when they were boyhood friends. The raft prank, the murder of my family and grandparents in Saraton, and the destruction of my drawings are just a few examples of our injuries. I am including the general mistreatment of Uncle Thomas by the king.

Many people are aware that Althea was adopted including some of the kitchen staff, and even the Long Bows. It will be common knowledge after I make a few public reductions on that list. On the day of the Knight Games two will die. The following day one will die. Two more days will bring about the death of the natural parents. The king will be eliminated when it suits me, but it will be after all the other participants are gone. These very public deaths will ignite the gossip, and it will not stop until it is common knowledge that the king adopted the princess.

Teas, specially concocted can end a life quickly and quite peacefully; even diluted tea can cause still birth.

Bettina

"Thanks to Quentin we know who the targets are, but we do not know the time and how. We are in serious trouble," the king said.

* * *Kendrick* * *

"Pssst. *Pssst.*" Althea picked up a pebble and tossed it at Kendrick. It struck Hunter, who looked to see where it had come from. The movement interrupted Kendrick's focus on the Knight Games.

The shadows hid the details of her face, but Kendrick sensed something was troubling her. When he was a few feet away, he saw the tears and watched as she sniffed daintily into a handkerchief. Without thinking, he placed his arm around her shoulders and directed her to a quieter area.

"What is the matter?" he whispered.

"I received disheartening news this morning," Althea replied.

"Is the king's condition worsening?"

"No! Quentin told me the archbishop has proof that I am the king's adopted daughter, and my natural mother is a farmer's wife."

"Oh that." He realized his mistake in that moment. But it was too late.

"*Oh that?* You...knew?!"

"Yes." He paused, and gazed eagerly into her eyes, for something, anything that would tell him that she would still be speaking to him. "I found out from Reginald after our last meeting at the grand curve. I was going to tell you at our next meeting.

Althea's eyes moved from his face. She held herself tightly and walked away from him toward the sunlight. But even then she struggled to stand still. He was more confused then when they first met at the market.

Minutes later she turned. But all Kendrick could see was her frown. She was unhappy with him.

Walking to her, he offered a hug of comfort. But she was quick to hold up her palms. His advance was halted.

"We have shared many secrets together. Why didn't you tell me? I have told you everything! And you cannot respect me enough to discuss this?"

"I attempted to contact you but ran into some trouble. If it is true, the facts would not change, regardless of when I told you."

"That's not the point. *You* knew and did not tell me." There was more than a trace of anger in her voice.

"I apologize."

"You cannot just apologize this away." Her eyes suddenly widened. "Who's Reginald?"

"Reginald Hamilton, Samantha's husband."

"Samantha who?"

"Samantha, your mother!"

"You—*knew my mother's name*—and did not tell me?"

"I'm sorry, Althea—I mean princess." He held his hands open towards her. "I underestimated the importance of this information...Please, I am sorry."

Three knights of the Long Bows approached the princess. She held up her hand. They stopped like trained dogs waiting for her command.

Kendrick reached for her right arm. The sound of swords scraping against sheath's brought silence to the staging area. He released her arm.

Her crimson face burned, and in that moment she slapped him.

"*I never want to see you again,*" she said.

* * Kendrick * *

Kendrick stood still for almost a minute feeling the sting of his cheek and the pounding of his heart. He felt alone and hollow as if a piece of his soul had left him. He wanted desperately to fix what he'd broken, but he didn't know how.

181

Five minutes later, Oscar returned. In ten minutes they would both be competing in the obstacle course. He pulled Kendrick aside and updated him on the archbishop's death and Bettina's disappearance.

There was no time for Kendrick to react. To feel. To do anything about his encounter with Althea. At the sound of the whistle, the obstacle course was announced and Oscar was filling him in on the details:

"That is what we know so far... We have assumed that Bettina has initiated her plan. It is the safest position for us to take. Son, I am sorry that you are involved in this tangled mess. But you are here and need to be prepared. Bettina's letter leads us to believe there are several people involved. I am surprised by the depth of the archbishop's revenge."

"What should I be looking for?" Kendrick asked.

"Think about hunting in reverse. If you were being hunted, where can you go to avoid the arrows? The Knight Games arena is safer than this staging area. You are less of a target in the obstacle course because there are ten participants at a time. The course obstacles provide some cover. It is possible they might attack you during the course, but I think they will attempt to remain incognito. We should get out front and stay there."

"Out front it is," Kendrick said. He paused for a few seconds feeling a depth of anxiousness that multiplied knowing that someone was out for his death.

The whistle tweeted three times, it was the third heat, and they were up. He exited staging with his father, Hunter, the sergeant, and six other competitors. When all ten participants were ready, a long, single whistle started the race.

Kendrick and Hunter were out in front in a few seconds. Oscar followed next. The gap between the leaders and seven other participants increased over the first three obstacles—log stairs, ladders, and the water tank. Kendrick caught Althea looking a couple of times at the ground in front of the podium. Kendrick weaved between the upright logs and created a lead of a few seconds. Hunter and Oscar collided entering the serpentine section.

Kendrick turned the corner and glanced back to see Hunter had fallen off and the sergeant was ahead of his father. He focused on the upcoming log jumble. Several upright logs of various heights were lined up about two feet apart.

He looked over his shoulder. No one was close. The last obstacle was a log swinging on ropes above a mud pit. Kendrick crossed the log and ran to the finish line. The crowd cheered as he crossed. Oscar had fallen off to seventh position.

Nine crossed the finish.

"Where is Hunter?" Kendrick asked.

"He stopped after the jumble, rubbing the back of his legs," Oscar replied.

"What happened to you?"

"I twisted my ankle when I jumped the water tank."

The sergeant walked by with blood on his hands.

"Sergeant, what happened?" Oscar asked.

"I tripped on the end of the last log ladder and cut them on the log when I fell."

"We should go rest before the archery finale," Oscar said.

There was an hour break while the arena was changed for the archery portion. The competitors had been whittled down from fifty-to-fifteen across the three events.

The competitors were scattered about in the staging area. There was little talking amongst the group as they were checking their bows, strings, and arrows.

Oscar pulled Kendrick off to the side.

"The archery competition is very open and you will be an easy target. I am going to withdraw from the last event and will be wandering throughout the arena. Keep your focus on the targets when you are shooting, and be alert to other activities between shots. Hopefully, you will finish in the top three." Oscar was silent for a few moments before he asked, "How are you feeling?"

"I will be fine," Kendrick replied.

"Your enthusiasm has tapered off since lunch."

Kendrick debated about how much to tell Father. Oscar had approved of Althea and Kendrick's relationship for tactical reasons, but not for romantic ones. "Althea slapped me."

Fatherly eyes burned into his. "Just as well. You two were not destined to be together—you are from different classes."

Kendrick lowered his voice, "She is Reginald and Samantha's child. Same class as us."

Oscar was quiet. He looked around. No one was near. "How did you find out?" he whispered.

"Father, I should not say. If I had not known before, Althea would have revealed the secret in our conversation at lunch."

"Do you know how she found out?"

"Quentin told her," Kendrick replied. "For such a big secret, many people appear to know about her adoption." Kendrick looked at the ground, scuffed the dirt with his boot, and rubbed the back of his neck. He wanted to know. *Had* to know. But how could he say it? How would he start?

He looked up at his father. The man was still staring into his eyes, concern written within. "What is it you want to ask?"

"Did you have anything to do with the adoption?" he asked.

* * *

Like the knife throwing competition, the first archery target was large and close. Each successive target

184

shrunk in diameter and moved further from the shooting line.

Twelve competitors had finished as Kendrick began. At each shot he used the time he needed to focus his mind. Between shots he looked around the arena for anything unusual. Through the first seven targets he was perfect.

In the distance, he saw his father's silhouette over target eight. In that split second his concentration was temporarily diverted causing him to release the arrow too soon. It hit the edge of the target. He would have to shoot the last two targets on center, only then would he be in contention for first place.

At target nine, his breathing slowed as he removed an arrow from the quiver. He set it against the string and rested on his front hand. A tingling sensation rushed throughout his body. He knew the arrow was on target the instant he'd released the string.

Target ten—the last competitive target of the day. Kendrick pulled the last arrow from his quiver, rested it on the string above the knot, brought the string back to his cheek, and slowed his breathing. He looked down the arrow shaft. The string slid off his fingers and propelled the arrow through the imagined tunnel to dead center.

A cheer rang out.

He collected his arrows from the targets, proud of his accomplishment, but worried he was being watched. Still, nothing had happened thus far, and maybe nothing would.

Two more contestants finished the archery participation ending the games.

As the judges added up the scores, the audience cheered, and moments later, three winners were brought out amid the darkening sky and cool breeze that signaled the beginning of a thunderstorm.

Althea descended the stairs from the podium with the medals and prizes. As she approached the three winners she avoided eye contact with Kendrick.

The third place medal was placed over the neck of the Long Bow winner, and she handed the man his prize— a pewter beer stein. She congratulated him then shook his hand.

Kendrick leaned over to receive his medal and it was if time stood still. Here, in the most favored moment of his lifetime, Althea stood in front of him, but he didn't know if he'd ever see her again. Look into her eyes. Touch her hand. He could feel the metal, the coldness of it as she reached over his neck. And in that moment he heard it, little more than a rush above his right ear, but a movement nonetheless.

Pushing the princess aside, he snatched the arrow with his right hand from the air.

The audience gasped, then cheered, their voices filling the arena like thousands of birds. Lightning flashed and a few seconds later thunder rumbled in the west.

Kendrick stepped in front of Althea, the arrow readied in his bow.

Suddenly, someone was yelling, running from the shadows down the ramp.

Let the Revenge Begin

* * *Oscar* * *

Oscar could smell rain as he investigated the far side of the arena, checking shadowed locations. He heard the gasp and cheers of the audience suddenly smothered by the thunder.

"Did you see him catch the arrow from mid-air?" he heard someone say.

He'd entered the seating area as Kendrick had stepped around the princess.

A few moments later, Hunter was seen running down the ramp from the shadows.

"You insignificant pretender! You must die!" Hunter yelled as he placed an arrow in his bow.

In a few seconds, Hunter would release another arrow. Oscar's pulse quickened and his mind raced to analyze his options in protecting his son. He clinched his fists and jaw as he realized he was unable to save his son from such a distance with patrons running through the arena avoiding the rain.

Running across the arena floor, time seemed to slow down. He felt every single drop of rain and pebble underfoot.

Althea, still behind Kendrick, was clinging to his waist, her long gown dripping at his feet. In the next moment, Kendrick's arrow must have been released, because it was suddenly penetrating Hunter's skin below the left lung

Hunter's arrow hit the arena dirt wildly. He pulled his knife, pushed the arrow through his back, cut the arrow shaft, and removed the shaft from his body. He replaced his knife—the whole process took only a few seconds. Then, he pulled another arrow from the quiver.

Oscar still didn't have a clear shot.

"Kendrick, he is reloading!" Oscar yelled. "Stop him!" Would Kendrick be hesitant? He hadn't been in a combat situation like this before, and Oscar wondered what he would do now.

Althea turned toward Oscar then back at Kendrick.

"Stop him!" Althea said.

The barb bladed arrow left Kendrick's bow, hurling through the air like a falcon diving on a mouse, stopping only as it slid through Hunter's right shoulder. Oscar was impressed—the arrow would be difficult to remove, and there would be someone to interrogate.

Oscar approached the awards location, his shoes caked with the moist arena soil. "Are you two all right?" he asked.

"Yes, I am fine. Thank you," Althea whispered while avoiding eye contact with Kendrick.

"Yes. I am good," Kendrick said.

Oscar signaled the Long Bows hidden in the corridors and crowd. Four dressed as civilians moved to protect the king and Quentin. Two more moved down the ramp to take Hunter into custody.

"I am not sure the princess was the target," Oscar said.

"Not the target?" Kendrick asked.

"I believe Hunter is a knight from Saraton. At that distance he would have the skill to strike Althea anywhere he chose. He would have shot her when she was giving the third place medal, walking across the arena floor, or conversing with a winner.

Kendrick moved to Althea's other side. Suddenly, an arrow passed through his quiver. He yelped. Kendrick bent over to pull the arrow from his thigh just as another arrow missed Kendrick's head by a few inches.

Oscar and Kendrick circled to protect the princess and Oscar determined the severity of Kendrick's wound. The arrowhead had not fully penetrated the skin.

Kendrick glanced over at him. "It stings quite a bit, from the rain I think."

The crowd crossing the arena floor had tapered off making the adjustment to safety that much easier. The arrows origin was in front of two of the arena access openings at the far end of the arena.

Two rogue Long Bow archers had turned and were running up the steps with their bows in hand.

"Flaming dragons!" Oscar started, stopping himself. "I just left there." He breathed heavily and turned to the sergeant. "Take care of the princess," he said, though thoughts of leaving Kendrick with the princess were dashed when he remembered Althea was upset with Kendrick. Changing his mind, he ordered the third place knight to accompany the sergeant. To Kendrick he said, "We must stop these assassins."

The rain had about emptied the stands as patrons held blankets over their heads running for shelter.

Another volley of arrows appeared from the shadows. Kendrick reached the bottom of the stairs and stepped side–to–side as he advanced up each stair. He would not have time to snatch another arrow from the air or dodge one. The rogue archer would have to wait until he was close. Four rows from the top he jumped from the stairs to the seats, and Oscar watched the arrow fly past him. A touch of air blew past his cheek along with an arrow over the thinning crowd, finally landing in the arena mud.

Thankful Kendrick had shown him a better way to climb the stairs, he pulled his knife as he skipped the last two stairs into the shadows.

Oscar was surprised. Standing before him was one of the two Long Bows who had claimed sickness during Althea's abduction. The rogue Long Bow had wide eyes, a clinched jaw, and stood against the back wall with his bow extended like a spear toward him.

The Long Bow made sweeping movements to hold him off. Concerned about his son and the time this could take, Oscar threw his knife at the spy. The handle's butt stuck the man between the eyes, causing him to fall. Two Long Bows collected the wobbling rogue knight by the arms. His pink face went white as his head fell forward.

The third Long Bow had arrived. "Captain Oscar, they have taken Kendrick as a hostage!" he reported.

"Where?"

"Two gates over."

Normally, Oscar was very composed during battle, but where Kendrick was involved his heart beat faster. He entered the dark corridor between the gates moving toward Kendrick's location, approaching like a cat stalking a bird. A lightning flash allowed him to see one of his Long Bows holding Kendrick at knifepoint. It made his stomach turn and he wiped his sweaty palms on his shirt.

"I want to talk to Oscar," the second spy demanded.

"He is on his way," came a voice outside the corridor.

Oscar was ten feet behind, waiting for another lightning strike.

"Kendrick," he whispered at the flash.

Kendrick went limp causing the spy to lose his grip and balance. His son spun around and drove his right fist up into the spy's jaw. Two of three Long Bow knights rushed to the spy and grabbed his arms. The spy vigorously resisted then wilted when the third knight struck the spy's head with his sword handle.

Oscar hugged his son. "Our work has just begun."

* * *Kendrick* * *

The thunderstorm had passed. Kendrick could smell the fresh rain. The low, dark clouds were followed by white high puffs floating slowly as the horizon cleared.

Oscar stopped Kendrick before they entered the jail.

"You have a choice. You can listen in on the interrogation because of your involvement, but I cannot have you do anything that distracts from my methods. Or, you can wait out here."

Kendrick nodded and they entered the jail. A spy sat in each of three corners of the main room guarded by two Long Bows each.

"Take those two in the back. Do not let them talk," Oscar ordered. He turned to Kendrick. "Put your weapons in the far corner. Then bandage his wounds. The bandages are just inside the door to the holding cell... Gentlemen, please take positions in the two remaining corners. And be prepared to shoot him," he said to the two knights.

"Were you a captain of the Saraton knights, or a soldier in their army?" he said, turning to Hunter.

"I was a sergeant in my king's service waiting for orders. You killed two of my comrades and my captain many years ago in a public execution," Hunter replied.

"I regret doing that, but orders are orders. You know what it is like—unpleasant tasks that have to be done for your king."

Oscar nodded to Kendrick to bandage the wounds. "We cannot have him bleed to death," he said, waving his hand in the general direction of Hunter's wound.

"Kendrick, since our first meeting, you have been an enormous pain in my life," Hunter said.

"How so?" Kendrick asked as he stopped wrapping the bandage around Hunter's shoulder.

"*Kendrick*, just bandage the wounds," Oscar said sternly as he pointed at the shoulder and side wounds.

"Yes, sir."

Oscar waited until Kendrick finished.

"We have options for extracting information from you. As we are in a hurry to know the truth, the list of methods is much shorter and usually requires escalating pain until we are satisfied you have told us the truth. You will be near death and likely put in the dungeon, forgotten. Your family will never know what happened to you."

Hunter lifted his eyebrows slightly. He seemed unconcerned.

"My preferred option is cutting off your fingers one knuckle at a time—that is up to twenty-eight chances for us to get satisfactory answers. I guess we could include your toes. They are harder to cut so we would take the whole toe—we are up to thirty-eight. Please take a moment to consider the pain you will feel today and the difficulty you will have without your fingers and toes."

Like a stone statue, Hunter's face was motionless.

The room was silent for what seemed like an eternity. Kendrick's heart was pumping; he was perspiring on his arms, palms, and back. *Would Father really cut off this man's fingers and toes?* The thought sent shivers up his spine.

"I know about the difficulty of living without fingers. You see my wife had a disease that made her joints inflexible. She could not dig vegetables from the ground, hold a fork, dress herself, or prepare food," Oscar said.

Kendrick turned away from Hunter and squeezed his eyes shut. He envisioned his hands without fingers. He thought of his mother, so sickly before her death...

"I just thought of a way to give us more chances to make us comfortable with your answers," Oscar continued. "We will pull your fingernails first, then hit your finger tips with a hammer. That gives us twenty more—we are up to fifty-eight opportunities to get to the truth." Oscar paused for a few moments. "The truth is a funny thing. You have the information we need, but we are not sure what the truth is. So...we will have to ask you several times to see if you are consistent."

Kendrick looked at the two Long Bows in the adjacent corners with their bows ready to draw if Hunter tried to escape. But the knights refused to make eye contact. *Was this truly what Father did for the king?*

He sat on a nearby chair looking at his father and Hunter. All was silent. Kendrick's stomach grumbled and his mouth felt dry. *Was Father going to do this in front of him?*

Finally, Hunter broke the silence. "I know what my fate is—painful lengthy interrogation, prison while you verify my story. Then I am executed. But, consider this option—I cooperate, you verify my story, if it is good you let me return to Saraton, and I will never leave there. I can give you valuable information. Besides, I do not want to be mutilated."

Kendrick tried to control his stomach. He was halfway off the chair, leaning in to see Hunter's and Oscar's faces. After a few seconds of silence, Kendrick focused on his father who slowly rubbed his index finger and thumb on his beard stubble.

"One lie and I will execute you myself."

Kendrick's eyes widened.

"We have met before," Kendrick said. "You are the leader of the ruffians that I knocked down when you were terrorizing Althea."

"Kendrick!" his father implored. But Kendrick's mind was elsewhere.

"Oscar, you have a clever son," Hunter said.

"Start with why you were terrorizing Althea," his father asked.

"The archbishop needed the law changed so a younger Quentin could take the throne." Hunter sat back in the chair and crossed his legs. "So we were to present ourselves as Saraton rebels, kidnap the princess, and hold her until the law changed. The archbishop's plan required us to demand other changes in the law, and the release of other Saraton spies as a diversion. She, the queen, and the king were to be poisoned a few months after Althea's return."

Kendrick took a deep breath. *Had his involvement really gone back that far?*

"Any other encounters with the princess?" Oscar asked.

"I hired three mercenary acquaintances to abduct her from the market to a waiting wagon. This was a scheme ordered by the exiled Saraton king. He wanted King Louis III to step down and surrender Manshire. The Saraton king died two months later."

"Why did you kill the captured abductor?"

"We thought he might talk. The conspiracy theories are thick here and could easily be connected to one of several rumored schemes."

"Kendrick was ambushed a few weeks ago. Do you know anything about that?" Oscar asked.

Kendrick leaned forward in his chair.

"Bettina offered us a small fortune to remove Kendrick—partly because she was jealous of Althea, and partly because he had rescued Althea at the big oak tree— a time when she fully supported the archbishop's plans. After a while, she grew impatient with the archbishop and his constantly changing plans. In several meetings with the archbishop she expressed frustration with the changing execution dates.

"When the archbishop sold his family's business they were both rich," he continued. "Now Bettina could afford to hire her own spies and soldiers. I used the same villains in the big oak tree blunder in case they were caught. They would be seen as motivated by revenge, and my action could not be traced back to Bettina."

"You were the one that hit Shorty with the rock?" Oscar asked.

"Yes."

"How did you get connected to the archbishop?"

"Through the librarian. Years ago, I had worked with him to coordinate the king's escape to exile. He knew of my training as a knight and offered to pay me to murder the archbishop, and any living relatives, at some future date. He introduced me to the archbishop so I could get close to him when the librarian was ready."

"Why didn't you return to Saraton?"

Hunter leaned forward in the chair, his forearm on his thigh.

"I received pay from the archbishop to be ready for his revenge plans, and would get paid for his demise. I could pack up my family in a day and return to Saraton in two. It was easy money."

"How many spies, knights, or soldiers make up the archbishop's private army?"

"Bettina, two Long Bows, and me." He paused, looked above Oscar's head, and tilted his head to the left. "There *might* be one more. That is all I know of."

"What do you know of Bettina's plan?" Oscar asked.

"Today was just the beginning. You and Kendrick were scheduled for today at the games. She wanted to maximize her success by first killing the two whom she thought could stop her. Bettina believed your continued involvement could dismantle her plans. She assumed correctly."

"And the others?" Oscar asked.

"Althea is to be poisoned soon. The Hamiltons are next, and I believe she plans to use Kendrick's knife. By the time the Hamiltons are discovered at their home, it will be hard to tell how long they have been dead, and it will look like Kendrick killed them before the Knight Games. Quentin will be poisoned a week later. Then finally the king will be poisoned. She hates that man and all those close to him. She hinted the schedule would have to be moved up to keep him from dying of natural causes."

Wow! Father had expertly used the power of suggestion. Like the ambusher's interrogation, his father hadn't inflicted much actual pain, but he'd made the prisoner believe he was capable and willing. *He wondered if his father had actually hurt anyone.*

"Kendrick, go to the barracks and get eight Long Bows then bring them back here," his father ordered.

Kendrick gathered his weapons from the far corner and exited the jail.

* * *Oscar* * *

Oscar felt Hunter had been truthful but that the entire story had not been revealed. He had to know about his son's safety.

"Now that Kendrick is gone, is he in any further danger?"

"Your son is safe as far as I know. Bettina is not a great strategist and I doubt she has a solid backup plan. I volunteered to take care of Kendrick, because he had bested me, a trained knight. I had a score to settle."

"I have heard several versions of the revenge plan. How confident are you with your version?" Oscar asked.

"It is Bettina. She could have lied to us to protect herself. You never know with her."

"Where is she now?"

"I would assume on her way to the Hamiltons. But I think she is overestimating her abilities. She is untrained, has to hide between here and their farm, she is on foot, probably weak from hunger, will battle with the husband to stab him, and so on. She is likely to be eaten by wolves before finding the Hamiltons. I would guess she is dead by now."

"You said there might be one more."

"At my last meeting with Bettina, she made an offhanded comment. 'Do not under estimate me', she said, after I told her the plan was weak. 'I have other means and ways you know not of.'"

"How had you planned to kill me?"

"During the archery portion of the Knight Games a stray arrow was going to find you. I manipulated my success at each event to keep close to you. I faked a pulled muscle. You could not be found but I knew where Kendrick was."

Oscar paced as he analyzed the information Hunter had provided. *What "other means" could Bettina have had?*

Kendrick and eight Long Bows returned. Oscar satisfied the Long Bows were loyal to the king, but was concerned with the number of people in the small room, the slippery mud collecting on the floor, and the proximity of weapons available to Hunter.

"Kendrick, tomorrow you are to direct these eight men to the Hamiltons farm and return with the family to the castle."

He heard the dull sliding sound of a knife against a leather sheath an instant before he saw the red throat of the gasping, gurgling, and wide-eyed Long Bow. Hunter was preparing to throw the knife at Kendrick when Oscar dove and knocked Kendrick out of the way. The knife hit the wall and fell to the dirty wooden floor.

Oscar spun to see Hunter removing the Long Bow's sword. "Stop him!" Oscar yelled.

Both corner Long Bows released their arrows. Hunter dropped the sword and fell to his knees. He stared at Kendrick for a few seconds, turned his gaze to Oscar, and nodded his head as if he were saying he conceded defeat to Oscar and Kendrick. Hunter slumped over then fell forward onto the floor. He was dead.

ANDEAN WHITE

Flaming Dragons

* Kendrick *

They left at sunrise. The sun's light illuminated the sky as Kendrick led the eight Long Bows to the Hamiltons. Alternating, they rode hard for ten minutes and slowed for five minutes to save the horses. The two-hour wagon ride was half the time on horseback.

As they cleared the trees, Kendrick saw the smoke. Had Bettina set the Hamiltons' farm on fire? He kicked the horse's haunches and it broke into a full run.

A black smoldering lump lay on the side of the road ahead. Kendrick couldn't make it out. At twenty feet, he slowed his horse to get a good look. It was a burned bear. *Odd.*

"We need to find the Hamiltons," he instructed the Long Bows knights.

The charred trees were a stark contrast to the soft grey smoke produced by the smoldering barn and house. Kendrick could hear the coughing of two knights who had just entered. The smell of burned hair was pungent near the barn.

"They are not in here," coughed a voice from the barn.

"The house is empty," yelled another knight.

* Bettina *

She felt like a rabbit that had lost its leg in a trap— slow careful movements needed to overcome her handicap. So far she had learned to avoid any flowered bush. Bees, she hated bees.

Spectators returning home from the Knight Games traveled by foot, horseback, carts, and wagons. She'd had to hide from each group, though the banter regarding the end of the games had many wondering if it was theatre or reality. One thing she'd been able to piece together, Kendrick and Oscar were still alive.

As she hid behind a large boulder, thundering hooves approached. Kendrick and eight Long Bows slowed their horses. "We are half way there," Kendrick said.

She wanted to scream, but knew it would attract unwelcomed attention. She settled for a physical silence as she pressed her fists against the crown of her head.

* * *Althea* * *

Althea gently stroked the red ribbon on the silver medal hanging off the handle of the beer stein. The sunrise cast an orange hue on everything in her room. Yesterday afternoon's *near death experience* had upset her—she hadn't eaten or slept.

Her mind skipped from the adoption story, the slapping of Kendrick, the snatched arrow, the arrow in Kendrick's thigh, and his ultimate disappearance. Regardless the slap she'd given him, he had risked his life for her with the same dedication as his father.

Many components of her life were rapidly traveling off course and Father's poor health was progressing. Words could not describe how she felt about his keeping the adoption from her. Bettina was still free to execute her assassination plan. Kendrick's whereabouts were unknown. Most of the men in her life had kept secrets from her. And she...she had to correct the situation and needed time alone—perhaps a dip in the cool water.

That morning Althea had taken the Long Bow disguise from the box in the closet. Using the back stairs leading to the stables, she'd requested a horse. A minute later, the horse had been ready to ride.

* * *Kendrick* * *

"There should be a set of footprints for a man and woman, and maybe two small girls," Kendrick said.

"Over here," yelled one of the knights. "I found footprints into the forest."

His heartbeat increased as he ran towards the forest's edge.

The tracks led into the forest. Six full steps for Reginald and five for Samantha, but no footprints for two children.

"Spread out and see if we can find them," Kendrick said. *Could Father be wrong? Or are the invaders not coming from the north? Maybe Saraton spies are behind these burnings.*

The forest thickened about thirty feet inside the tree line. The small stream watered the nearby trees and a few young willows. Fallen trees had been cleared for firewood. A carpet of pine needles cushioned their steps.

They had searched for ten minutes when Reginald appeared from behind a patch of willows along the stream. Sweat, dirt, and small leaves sprouted within his newly ripped clothes. Twigs stuck inside his beard, and his hands and forearms were marked with scratches from thorny bushes. Blinking rapidly he scanned the area, jerking toward every noise.

"Kendrick?" Reginald asked. He held Kendrick for an extended hug.

"Yes. Reginald, we are happy to see you. Where is your family?"

"In the cave a few yards back."

"What happened?" he asked.

Reginald led the way to the cave. "It hit us about half an hour after sunrise. There was an awful sound then the barn began to burn," he said. "Here is the cave." He knelt by a bitter berry bush. "Samantha, it is Reginald."

The twins came out from behind the bush followed by Samantha. They held each other tightly for a few moments as the smoke started to thin.

"Father, there were spiders in the cave," Elsa said.

"Big ugly black ones," Erma added.

"Is *it* gone?" Samantha asked. Alternately, she rubbed her forearms and had yet to wipe the tear tracks from her pale cheeks.

"I think so. It is quiet."

"Did we lose the house, too?"

"Yes. I looked after we were in the forest."

"Why us? Why did *it* pick us?" Samantha asked. Tears began to flow.

"Reginald, what is *it*?" Kendrick asked.

"A dragon!"

* * *Oscar* * *

Althea flinched at the sound of footprints.

"Oscar, you followed me?"

"Yes, your safety is my responsibility. May I ask why you are taking such a great risk?"

"I need time to think. Yesterday included too many disturbing activities, and more challenging issues are on the horizon. I have to put everything in perspective," Althea said. "Did you know Kendrick and I met here weekly?"

"I suspected, until Kendrick confirmed it after the ambush. How can I help?" He knelt down by her side. "If you want to be alone, I can wait with the horses." She ran her fingers through her windblown hair, and took a deep breath.

"Why did Father keep my adoption from me?" she asked.

"He was trying to minimize the number of people who knew," Oscar replied. He sat beside her on the rock.

"Sounds like he wasn't very successful with that." Althea paused and Oscar noticed her eyes were welling with tears. "More specifically, why didn't he tell me sometime during these past few years?"

"Would it have made a difference?" Oscar asked. "I mean, would it have really mattered? You are still next in line for the throne. Quentin hasn't gotten any older. The archbishop's revenge plan would have been appropriated by Bettina regardless of your knowledge."

"That's the same response I received from Kendrick."

"What is going on between you and Kendrick? If you do not mind my asking," Oscar said.

Althea removed her feet from the stream and turned to face Oscar. "I am angry with him for not telling me that he knew about my adoption. I have told him everything...well, almost everything."

"So you have secrets, too," he said, winking. "I am not endorsing or discouraging your relationship. But to give you more information, he planned to tell you at your next grand curve meeting."

"Well, I have ruined any hope of ever being with Kendrick."

"It is just as well. You are royalty, we are servants."

"Kendrick is honest, thoughtful, considerate, and trustworthy. He saved my life that night by the big oak tree. He fought the ruffians, fed me, ran to protect me when I screamed, offered to be a diversion; he was a gentleman the entire time. He gave me this red stone." She held it out for him to see. It was small and glittered within her delicate hand. "It has comforted me on several occasions. I think I am in love with him."

Oscar wanted the best for them, but he wasn't sure if the answer meant a *shared* best. He swallowed twice to clear his throat, and then he tried to speak softly, with understanding, the same way a father would speak to comfort a daughter.

"Althea, you need to know about the king's decision. Saraton was placing spies and assassins in Manshire preparing to take over the country. Your father ordered us to spy on them and we found horrible conditions there. People were enslaved on their own farms. Barns were turned into quarters for the workers. Their meals were a watery broth. Clothes were mere rags. Fallen workers were left to die in the fields. And their king lived in lavish luxury."

"I did not know," Althea said.

"After four of your mother's babies died, we concocted a plan to substitute a child from Manshire if the fifth one was also delivered dead. The substitute was you. Now there was an heir to the throne. The king needed a plan to prevent a disorganized Manshire from falling into the hands of Saraton spies waiting for direction from the exiled king."

"Is this a concern now?"

"No. It was a big problem around the time of your birth," Oscar replied, touching her hand.

* * Bettina * *

Bettina was dressed in the rabbit coat, hat, and gloves she'd stolen from the maids' quarters. She had wanted matching sable attire to let the Hamiltons know someone, not just anyone, was killing them.

From her position behind the rock wall on the north edge of the property, she listened.

"As soon as the wagon is loaded, we are going back to the castle," said a deep voice, probably a Long Bow.

"How soon?"

"Not sure."

"It would go faster if we all pitched in."

"It would go faster if they were not sifting through every ash pile. We are on guard duty. They are loading the wagon. We should keep moving."

The crunch of fallen leaves filled her ears as the men walked off. There would be another detour on her revenge journey—the Hamiltons were moving to the castle. She wanted to scream but muzzled the yell. Her face flushed red as she shook both fists and bit her lower lip.

Another crunch of leaves.

"It flew off in the direction of Oscar's house," someone said.

"The devastation is unbelievable here. I wonder if it is the same everywhere."

"Have you noticed Kendrick has been preoccupied since hearing the beast flew off?"

"Yes."

Preoccupied? It was obvious she needed another plan.

* * Kendrick * *

The Long Bows had doused the small fires in the barn and house. A layer of soot covered everything. Two knights buried the charred body of the milk cow. One knight had started collecting the carrots and potatoes protected by the dirt.

"It was big and loud," said Erma

"And it was taller than the barn," Elsa added.

"Girls, your mother needs you to help gather some fire wood," Reginald said. The twins pouted and walked to Samantha.

"Tell us about the dragon," Kendrick asked.

"Like Elsa said, it was taller than the barn standing on its hind legs," Reginald said. "It roared and bobbed its neck three times before fire came out of its mouth. It was methodical. The trees, shrubs, and garden were the first to burn. The barn door was knocked down with a couple of swings from the beast's spade like tail. As the animals came out, it sorted them by size, after it broke their necks. It set the barn ablaze. The dragon turned toward the house and stretched its neck. Suddenly, a growling bear appeared from the woods. The beast stepped around in a circle and released fire. While it faced away from the house, we ran into the forest. The dragon ignited the house then flew off in the direction of your farm."

"The past two days have been very difficult. Bettina, the archbishop's niece," Kendrick said, "poisoned the archbishop, and paid former Saraton knights to assassinate the royal family and a few others. We learned yesterday she was coming here." He changed the subject as the twins came close. "I am going home to check on our place."

* * Bettina * *

The three-legged rabbit image was active again. Slowly, moving undercover toward the trail to Oscar's farm, commands could be heard, horses whinnied, and Samantha called the girls.

The Hamiltons were on their way to the castle.

Once, out of sight, Bettina grimaced as her hunger pains demanded satisfaction. Food was her first priority. Searching the empty barn for burned animals, she retrieved a couple of charred eggs from the bottom of the chicken coop, struck an egg on the corner of a burnt board, peeled the egg's shell, and sucked out the spongy undesirable mess inside. The second egg was a bit harder and more to her liking.

Dropping the shell pieces, she followed the rutted trail after Kendrick. The news of a dragon would divert attention from her. Maybe she could use the diversion to enhance her new plan.

* * Kendrick * *

Kendrick rode hard to the farm. The smell of smoke grew as he neared. When he exited the curve in the road, he could see the smoking barn and house. He dismounted the grey horse and watched from a distance. His family home was gone, covered with ash.

As the small fires continued to burn, twice Kendrick's unsettled stomach nearly lost its contents. He tried to think of the happy times he'd had there, but it hardly eased his mind of the total loss.

An hour later, thin smoke rose from the last of the small fires. He walked to the house. The window planters that had been filled with colorful flowers five days ago were blackened and dusted in grey soot. The fruit trees looked like a large version of the window boxes. Uncut grass, and this year's new roof, had been trampled by the dragon's large feet and burned around the edges near the house and barn. The blackened roses were eerily frozen in full bloom on the stems and highlighted with light grey soot.

Looking through the window, everything inside was blackened or burned—cinders covered the central fireplace. He could feel the heat coming from inside. The roof had collapsed. The interior walls were blackened. He moved to the barn and looked through the side door. It was the same as the house. The goat and all the chickens were gone.

He walked to the grass still pushing a bit of green through and fell to his knees and prayed. *Lord, thank you for the wonderful life Mother, Father and I enjoyed here. Please give me the knowledge to understand why we lost our house, and the hope to believe this is part of some master plan. I ask that you be with Father and I through these troubled times. May we conduct ourselves in a manner that pleases You. Amen.*

Opening his eyes he blinked, the firewood stacks were the only things left untouched—he would rest there tonight. He was exhausted from the Knight Games anyway, the full-time effort of trying to protect the princess, the interrogation, and the burned farm—an enormous loss that filled his soul. All the joy he'd experienced from inside his home seemed like a long ago memory.

The long shadows covered the barn and house. The pink, blue, purple, and yellow clouds were thinly stretched across the sky at sunset. The smell of the burned buildings lingered in the air. The cool static air coaxed Kendrick to sleep.

Only a few seconds separated Bettina on Draco, the dragon, from Kendrick atop Pegasus, the flying horse.

Draco also carried Althea—her wrists bound with heavy rope.

Their chase was burdensome. With a whistle, Kendrick guided Pegasus above Draco and directed him to dive.

Kendrick leaned over.

He attempted to pluck Althea off Draco as they flew by, but Bettina had anticipated his maneuver. She pulled the reins to slow Draco, and Pegasus passed in front of the dragon like a hawk diving on a ground squirrel.

In the next instant, Pegasus flew behind and under Draco.

Kendrick signaled Althea to jump. She rolled backwards off Draco.

*He caught her by the rope
between her wrists and lifted her onto
the back of the flying horse.
Bettina, holding Kendrick's knife,
guided Draco toward Althea...*

His eyes opened. It was dark. Something made a crashing noise—maybe a piece of the barn had fallen. His heart beat rapidly and beads of perspiration formed on his forehead. He felt as if something, or someone was there. Perhaps the dream was real? His senses told him no, that a dream could never be reality, but could it? Did dreams predict the future? Would he one day be flying through the air on a winged horse saving Althea?

* * *

The shadow from the hill east of the farm crept across the burned and disheveled garden, the patch of grass, and finally reached Kendrick sleeping on the woodpile.

Typically, he would rise right after opening his eyes, but today he lay there for several minutes, his mind drifting from the Knight Games contest, Althea's slap, protecting her, the arrow in the thigh, the interrogation, racing through the country, the Hamiltons smoldering farm, to the surprise of a dragon.

He took a deep breath. The dry, stale smell of the burned-out barn and house focused his attention like a slap in the face. Like Althea's slap, it meant a dramatic change in his future.

It was at this home that Mother had taught him to read, cook, plant, harvest, and play checkers. Here, he'd received hugs for his efforts, and chastisements to do better.

He slid off the stacked wood and stretched as he walked around. At the back of the house, he found the makeshift archery range Father had cleared for him—the target still hung on the tree. It was here, and at the family table, that Father had taught him about fate, following through on commitments, being a good friend, giving his best effort, and finishing anything he started.

Somewhere in his thoughts was something nagging at him. The slap? The burned farm? The dragon? He interlaced his fingers at the back of his neck, and silently shook his head. What had been the most disturbing thing from the last few days?

The interrogation!

Had Father been trying to teach him a lesson? Had Father hoped the experience would persuade him to seek other non-Long Bow employment? Or was he teaching Kendrick that actions had consequences?

Now that he had identified the source, it was like a tune from the market playing over and over in his mind. He considered his father's technique of slowly guiding the prisoner's thoughts, and escalating the prisoner's focus on the potential pain. He compared it to the ambush interrogation of Martin.

Father had used the power of suggestion to focus each prisoner on the painful process they faced. He was very patient—giving the prisoner plenty of time to think about their dilemma. Visual imagery provided the captive with a future vision of hope, if only temporarily.

Now, what about the rest of his life?

Last Commands

As Althea slept, Oscar watched. It was dark, and the conversation had stopped as she'd fallen asleep. They would stay the night at the grand curve.

He unsaddled the horses, feeling a guilty shiver sneak up his spine as he laid the saddle blankets on Althea. Yes, she was an attractive young woman. He'd had more significant moments with her than she'd probably with the king. She was like a daughter to him. He was envious of Kendrick. He wanted to be twenty years younger meeting Abbey at the market, walking in the snow, and spending time at the grand curve...

* * *

It was a clear morning. Althea sat straight in the saddle looking up the road. Her bounce in the saddle was in perfect rhythm with the horse's gait. Her hands gently held the reins as she directed the horse.

"It's a lovely morning," Althea said.

"You are in better spirits today," Oscar replied.

"Yes. Thanks to you I have a new perspective on secrets...and that things are not always as they appear to be." She paused. "Oscar, I would like to apologize to Kendrick for slapping him. May I continue to see him?"

"You will soon be queen, I cannot stop you. But, please be sure of where this may go. I do not want to see either of you hurt."

They rode in silence until they arrived at the castle. Across the river bridge they saw the sergeant waving them to hurry.

They crossed the moat's drawbridge. The clumping of the horses' hooves overcame the sound of the sergeant's voice.

"Oscar. Althea. Hurry," the sergeant breathed heavily. "The king is very sick and has been asking for you since last night. I could not find either of you."

A Long Bow knight took their horses as they ran up the steps to the king's bedroom. Oscar opened the door for Althea and waited outside.

"Father, are you awake?"

"Yes, Althea. Just resting my eyes," King Louis said. His airy voice was hard to hear.

"How are you feeling?"

"Not so good. This disease has finally caught up with me." He rested his eyes for a few seconds. "It is time for you to be queen."

"Oh, Father." She held his hand. A tear formed at the bottom of her left eye.

"No tears. You will be the queen tomorrow and must be strong."

"Yes, sir."

Oscar watched and listened through the nearly closed door. The king sat up, slowly, like any man. But he was an old and sickly man and suddenly, Oscar knew he had few days left.

"The list of people that know you are adopted and would use it against you has become quite short. For a time, when you were in your early teens, I thought everyone was going to find out. Regardless, you have the knowledge of how to handle the adoption should it come up. Your mother, the queen, has left a note for you in the Bible in her office. Her last wish for me was to let only you read it."

"I will read it later. Now it is time to be with you."

The king coughed for over a minute, covering his mouth with a blood stained handkerchief.

"Althea, your training has prepared you to be queen. Listen to your heart—something I should have done more of." He paused to take a deep breath. "Oscar come-in, please."

"Yes, my king."

"Althea, Oscar is a true and trusted friend first, and captain of the Long Bows second. I have found his advice to be trustworthy. You can discuss anything with him. But now...now I am feeling weak and want to discuss the coronation," the king said. "Usually, there is a ninety day mourning period for the former king before the coronation which is a two day event. We will dispense with that, as I am still alive. I have arranged for the coronation to take place tomorrow. I do not have many days left. The priest can conduct the proceedings. Shorten your speech as I cannot sit long."

"And Quentin?" Oscar asked.

"He should be seated on the first bench next to me," the king replied. "I had a nice talk with Quentin yesterday. When I discussed Althea as queen he informed me he wanted to become the archbishop for Manshire after he completes his tours as vicar and priest. Quentin thinks he can help more people one-on-one. He will be studying here, then at the diocese for the next four years."

ANDEAN WHITE

Dragon Quest

* * *Kendrick* * *

Kendrick rummaged through the ashes looking for anything salvageable, wondering what he was to do with the rest of his life. He had lost the family home, as well as Althea, and his father was discouraging his Long Bow dream.

The custom spoon Kendrick had made for his mother triggered a novel thought—with the house and barn gone, he was not hindered by any commitments. But what if no one needed him? That thought made his pulse quicken, along with a burst of nervous energy that traveled to every part of his body.

He completed his scavenger hunt of the house and barn. The small treasures were stored in the cast iron kettle—Mother's cherished gift from he and his father. Mother's custom spoon, a small hand mirror, and similar items had been placed in a clay pot. Kendrick rested the kettle and clay pot by the barn, stacked firewood around them, and sprinkled ash on the pile.

He thought of the week he'd started helping Mother, the knife gifted to him, and the winter he'd dug snow to move Mother to the barn. Father was outdoors in that storm at the end of his invaders from the north assignment. Walking to the horse, he realized that slaying the dragon was the answer. He would end the rumors of the northern invaders and show his value to the Long Bows. Father would not, could not, refuse him then as a Long Bow.

He disassembled the wood stack and added a piece of wood with a carved note to the collection, then reassembled the woodpile. He walked out to the pasture and rubbed the horse's front shoulder. A short rope placed about the neck guided the horse. The blanket used overnight as a pillow was unrolled and repositioned on the horse. The saddle, tossed on its back, was cinched in place.

A strange tingling up his spine. Scratching the back of his neck, he searched the surrounding area, slowly scanning the edge of the thick forest and large boulders, and leaned to look along the side of the house. He saw nothing unusual, but he felt something...

He mounted the horse and rode off to the eastern mountains.

* * Bettina * *

The night had been cold, and she was happy to be wearing her stolen rabbit coat. Watching Kendrick from a brush thicket, she found his actions strange. He entered the house, and a few minutes later exited with a kettle. He wiped soot off several small items, dug up some pots, placed the small items in the kettle and pots, hid the items in a woodpile, and rode off.

Bettina walked directly to the small woodpile. Carefully, she removed the dusty logs, clay pot, and iron kettle, smiling at the array of small items he had saved in the two vessels. She found the wooden note.

* * *Althea* * *

The assembly hall had been transformed. The grey drapes had been replaced with blue–green. Four fine oak benches had been placed near the front for invited guests. The remainder of the hall was standing room only. The throne had been moved from the king's office to the stage. Ropes tied between ten posts created a corridor that ran through the center of the room from the storage room at the rear.

The irony of waiting in the storage room made her smile. She was being stored with broken chairs, wash buckets, brooms, and washing rags until she was needed. An odd combination of soap and musty curtain smells filled the room along with the acrid aroma from the two oil-burning lamps. The ramshackle stack of broken chairs was layered with dust.

Peeking through the slightly opened door Althea could see her future subjects—all dressed in fine clothes.

A tingling sensation originated at her heart and instantly reached her extremities. Joy, confidence, fear, sadness, and excitement flashed within her mind. She had been trained all her life for this moment. She thought the full coronation would be easy like a spring breeze through the castle. She was surprised her hands were shaking, and her simpler speech was a jumbled nightmare: *I am interested in your ideas for improving our country. We are not a rich country, but we are a happy country.* She wiped the beads of sweat forming on her forehead.

"Relax, Althea," Father said nearby. "In fifteen minutes you will be queen of Manshire. And ironically, I will be one of your subjects."

Althea gazed into her father's eyes—they seemed sad. She smiled at him. Flashbacks of the many hours Father had spent teaching her filled her heart with joy.

A trumpet blared. The ceremony had begun.

"It is time," the priest said.

The priest exited the storage room, followed by two young teenage escorts dressed in gold and white striped shirts, green tights, and feathered hats carrying the scepter and an empty purple pillow. The king left the room next. He was stooped over. His once full-length blue cape now dusted the floor. Occasionally, he steadied his crown, which had been sized to fit Althea, and was now much too small for him. Two medium sapphires flanked the larger center emerald mounted in the gold headband.

When he reached the first step to the stage, King Louis III bowed to the priest. The priest approached, removed the crown, and placed it on the empty pillow. The trumpet bugled.

"Please welcome Princess Althea," the priest said.

Althea wore Queen Francine's shortened royal cape—blue with green fringe. She entered the assembly hall to cheers and applause, while a quartet of two violins and two cellos played in the background. People reached out their hands. Althea touched many of them as she walked down the corridor. When she reached the front, she hugged Father and Quentin. She proceeded along the first bench and hugged Oscar.

"Where is Kendrick?" she whispered.

"Uncertain, but I hope he is at home," Oscar replied.

She paused for a moment before returning to the rope corridor. Althea stepped up the three stairs. One of the escorts placed a knee pillow on the floor. She knelt before the priest. He opened the Bible and read a passage from Psalms *"The Lord is my shepherd...Yea, though I walk through the valley of the shadow of death, I will fear no evil...For thou art with me...my cup runneth over."*

The priest anointed her with oil. Althea rose and walked to the throne. The priest removed the crown from the pillow and placed it on her head. He handed her the scepter.

"I present to you Queen Althea the first, of Manshire."

Applause erupted like hundreds of dove wings. Father stood. He vigorously clapped and a smile revealed his pride, though several times he'd had to steady himself on the rope corridor post.

Suddenly, a wonderful aroma drifted up from the kitchen, a combination of pasty and cinnamon reminding

218

Althea of the birthday and holiday parties, lunches with Mother at the market, and Kendrick.

After a minute of silence at the podium she extended her hands for quiet. Father had advised her to speak loudly.

> *"Thank you for your kind support. I look forward to meeting each of you at the ball tonight...I am interested in your ideas for improving our country...We are not a rich country, but we are a happy country. We live good lives and enjoy many pleasures not afforded other countries...I hope I can continue the good work of my father. Thank you."*

Queen Althea walked to the center of the stage. As the crowd applauded, Father and Oscar's eyes shone bright with tears. Quentin smiled at her as he clapped.

With a renewed hope, made possible by those who loved and accepted her, she walked off the stage and down the rope corridor, touching as many hands as possible.

She proceeded to the office that had been Father's, and embraced him and Oscar. The sergeant gave her a royal salute. She took the chair behind the desk that she suddenly realized needed some adjusting for her shorter legs. Former King Louis smiled as he sat.

"Louis, you never hugged me when we met. I like this better," Oscar said.

"You never called me Louis." His hands cupped around his nose while coughing.

"You were always king."

Althea smiled over at her father, looked for the mallet, and finding it, set the crown on the desk.

"Gentlemen, I want to form a search party for Kendrick," Queen Althea said. She looked at Oscar. "I know your feelings, but I need him."

Oscar instinctively turned to Louis.

"She is the queen," Louis said to his unasked question.

Oscar stood and bowed his head slightly at Althea. "Very well, your majesty. We shall leave at dawn. Unless your highness wants to leave later."

"No, no. This is your detail. I will not hold you up." She turned her attention from Oscar to the group. "Anything else? Gentlemen, enjoy tonight's coronation party."

* * Kendrick * *

Yesterday's travel was easy. The horse had been set free to roam the meadow. Traversing the mountains meant no trails or roads for the remainder of this journey.

For greater ease in climbing, Kendrick had taken his father's advice and hung his weapons on his belt. It felt awkward having the extra weight hanging on his waist, but his hands were free.

It was a difficult day. Twice he'd had to backtrack from a cliff he could not scale. His fingertips were sore from climbing, and blisters had formed on his feet from his too-large boots.

As he rested on the edge of a clearing, a large shadow passed over him. A hint of nervous satisfaction passed up his spine when he realized the dragon flew in the same direction as his travel.

The clearing gave him more skyline to observe the dragon than if he had been in the thick forest surrounding him. It was larger than his imagination, and glided through the air with ease. A single flap of its wings seemed to propel it for miles. The body was twice as long as a horse, and the tail was the same length with a diamond shaped spade at the end. The wings reminded Kendrick of quilts being stretched on a frame for sale at the market. Its muscular back legs were tucked behind his body and the short front legs were stuck against the torso. The head appeared two times larger than a bull's.

A goat's head hung out of its mouth. Kendrick believed the dragon had returned from one of its *invasions*. Before a mountaintop blocked his view, the beast's wings formed a "V" shape as it prepared to land. He could be there in a few days' journey.

As the sun would be setting soon, he stopped to make camp before exiting the forest. A small, crackling campfire with double rock rings cooked the dove and kept him warm. The roasting dove had a sweeter aroma than chicken, but lacked enough meat for his rumbling belly. It left him wishing for more.

* * *Oscar* * *

Oscar led the group at a quick pace. He hoped to find Kendrick tending the farm. With any luck, Reginald's suggestion about which direction the dragon flew from the Hamiltons would be seen as a mistake.

He had to slow the horse to make the sharp turn at the entry to his side road. The rest of the group managed to avoid collision. After crossing the short bridge over the brook, a slight smoky smell caused him to kick the horse in the haunches. Oscar imagined that the house and barn looked like the others he'd seen the last few months— irregular wall heights with the lingering smell of smoke.

As he flew past the line of berry bushes on the curve to his house, his stomach turned. The burned buildings came into view and the smoky odor filled his lungs. Scanning the open area around the house, barn, and garden, he wondered if Kendrick was there. What would he do if he found his son's body?

Oscar dismounted his horse, dropped the reins, and ran toward the house. Opening the door slowly and carefully moving pieces of the fallen roof to see if it had caught his son, he called out, "Kendrick!"

Wiping the soot from his shoulders and sleeves he hurried to the barn. The barn contained flammable items like hay and was nearly gutted. Cold ash were piled on the dirt floor. He was relieved that he hadn't found Kendrick and hoped no one else had either.

Leaving the barn, memories flooded his mind.

He saw her crying in the garden, the colorful window boxes, the rich green colors of the vegetable garden, the pleasant aroma of the rose bushes behind the house, the sweet taste of the autumn apples, training Kendrick at the archery target...

Oscar stopped and sat on the narrow stump of the old pine tree. He recalled that Abbey had cut it down because the needles soured the bedding soil in that corner of the garden. His hands rested on his knees, leaving dark smudges on his pant legs. He stared at the ground. Tears slowly trickled down his nose and made a small clicking noise when they hit the burned leaves.

Althea walked over and rested her hand on Oscar's back. "It is surprisingly more devastating when it is your home," he said.

"This is the first burned home I have seen," she began, her hand still resting on his back. "And now I understand the resources Father put into the problems of the northern invaders."

A piece of the barn wall fell. It sounded like a slap when it reached the ground. A startled Oscar noticed the odd small stack of firewood, blackened personal items, clay pot, and kettle scattered by the barn. Oscar suspected the stash had something to do with Kendrick— perhaps these items were something he wanted to hide— though he couldn't be sure.

A Long Bow approached holding a flat piece of wood, which he handed to Oscar. Carved into the surface was *Father, I have decided to end the reign of this dragon. It has tormented too many people. Kendrick.*

Why had the carved note been separated from the other items he'd discovered by the destroyed barn? This question brought about two other questions he couldn't answer. Had someone beaten him to the pile? And if so, who was it?"

* * *

"Gather around," Oscar commanded. "The trail separates about halfway to the mountains. We will break up into three groups—northeast, southeast, and due east. Search for five days then return to the castle. Althea, come with me." *Oscar hoped Althea had not caught his indiscretion of not addressing her as Queen in public.*

Continuing to press forward, Oscar led his group. By late evening, they had come across a saddled horse roaming in the meadow. The saddle blanket had the king's crest. The leather armor extension had been cut from the saddle.

"We will rest here tonight. Kendrick must be on foot."

As Queen Althea watched the full moon rising in the east while the Long Bows established camp, one of the men asked, "Do you think she is really dead?"

"She cannot be alive. The wolves are more active in the lower lands this time of year," suggested another Long Bow.

"The temperature is near freezing at night. She probably froze to death," added a third.

Was she really dead?

* * Bettina * *

The rumble of horses approached. Bettina scanned the area for a place to hide. The ground rumbled as the team of Long Bows led by Oscar and Althea galloped at full speed.

A horse would fulfill her current wish. Her feet were swelling in her shoes, and with every step the blister on her heel delivered sharp pain. If only she had made it to the Hamiltons before Kendrick and the rescue team, she could have had that horse.

Her coat and gloves were dirty and burs covered the hem. She'd stopped to remove them, when suddenly a high-pitched squeal escaped from underneath a small bush. With Kendrick's knife in hand, she pressed the branches back to see a small rabbit, its hind feet caught in a snare trap. Their eyes met. The bunny tried to wiggle free. Bettina shoved the knife into its belly.

Unable to start a fire even if she had flint or kindling, she was hungry, weak, but determined in her revenge. So with great care she ate the stringy, cold, and distasteful meat. It rumbled in her stomach like a roaring fire in winter. She wiped her hands and mouth on the large sleeves of her coat and stood.

With fourteen sets of tracks, the trail was easy to follow. With her belly filled, she tried to focus on the task at hand. By late afternoon, when the sun was high and her throat sticky and dry, she'd almost given up when she saw the once full group had gone their separate ways. The group heading due east appeared to have more tracks— *Probably the group protecting the queen,* she reasoned with herself.

* * Kendrick * *

The next morning, Kendrick was awakened by the screech of the dragon, and his burning, pulsating thigh.

Carefully, he got up from another night sleeping on the ground. He stretched to relieve his sore muscles.

After an hour of climbing over large boulders, Kendrick estimated he had travelled about a mile and was now above the tree line, which meant no birds, no roots, and no grass.

He was thankful that the rest of today's journey appeared to be downhill and back into the forest. His leather boots had begun to fray from the constant rubbing on the jagged rocks.

By mid-morning the two-hundred-foot cliff ledge had narrowed to five feet. He'd happened upon a large tan and grey boulder on the left side of the path, wedged between two walls. Water slowly trickled around its edges. From three-quarters of the way up the left side water dripped into a gravel bowl and disappeared. The top of the wedged rock sloped up to the right. Water soaked the bottom half of the adjoining seam and ran under the landslide of strawberry to melon-sized rocks, then vanished.

If he could not climb the rockslide he would have to backtrack.

The rocks and gravel moved under his weight, and twice the effort was needed to navigate the slide. Several times the loose stones gave way, and he found himself lying flat on the rockslide, igniting the burning in his thigh. Twice, his foot jerked to a sudden stop after rapidly sliding down the sword sheath that had slid underfoot. He was grateful when his hand had grasped the rock's top. He pulled himself onto the edge of the rock and sat until his thigh cooled. Kendrick lowered his head and whispered, "Thank you."

The pool of warm slick water was filled by an artesian spring bubbling from beneath a large stone covered with apple-sized rocks. Behind the spring a wide belt of large boulders offered a stark backdrop to the pond area. The ground around the pond was covered with a thick, soft, green grass. The trees were young—thick below the spring and much thinner above the spring. Bunches of yellow and blue flowers grew inside the tree line. Kendrick thought he had found Heaven.

He drank small amounts of water for ten minutes, then took off his clothes and dove in.

Kendrick spent half a day around the pool. He carved wooden soles to tie on the bottom of his boots. He shot a rabbit and had lunch.

Rested, he decided to travel as far as possible. He walked for four hours, made camp, and built a bed of long pine needles and grass. He felt good. While eating roots and berries for dinner, he heard a screech similar to what had awoke him in the morning. *He must be close...*

The stories his mother had told him were offered in truth, but reality was revealing a different twist. Not all the dragons were slain during the purge fifty years ago. The drunken farmers probably heard the dragon's screech. The random rumors of momentary sightings above the forests treetops were likely true.

His knowledge of dragons was limited, but perhaps he knew enough—had to know enough.

Before resting, he cut ten wedges of wood and placed them in his burlap sack, watching the moon appear on the eastern horizon. The stars and constellations were not visible in the western sky as a storm moved in.

Kendrick thought of the moment he'd have to face the beast—the moment reality would be in front of him and he'd have to face his fear. His heart pounded.

To calm his mind he began to think again of his father and Althea, only then did he sleep, and dream.

Bettina, who was on Draco and aiming Kendrick's knife, dived at Althea.

He directed Pegasus to dive to the right.

Suddenly the maneuver backfired.

The knife cut the shoulder of the hand holding the rope between Althea's wrists.

Kendrick had to fight off the stinging pain. As Draco flew by the dragon slapped him with the spade of his tail.

Kendrick shook his head hoping to fend off the instinct to pass out.

He was thankful for the cool air.

When Kendrick pulled her upright,

Althea closed her eyes and silenced a groan as the rope scuffed her wrists.

She pressed her hand on his warm, bloody shoulder.

Now Bettina was coming around for another pass.

And with each pass the sky alternated between day and night.

"Althea, how do you feel about using Bettina to cut the rope between your hands?"

"It's a little risky. I think I can do it with your help..."

Lightning struck the rocky outcropping above, waking Kendrick. Sweat soaked his shirt. His heart beat heavily.

He bumped his thigh on the edge of the fallen tree next to where he slept. The tears were instant, and intense pain sent him to the ground on his hands and knees. He muffled the scream with his hand, but remained on the ground, waiting for the pain to subside.

The slow rain reminded him of the gentle rhythm of ice melting in early spring. Kendrick held his sack above his head. The smell of fresh rain brought back memories of playing checkers with Mother to pass the time during a storm. A sense of nostalgia stirred his confidence. He stood and stared at the silhouette of the butte. Another flash of lightning struck and a loud screech echoed through the mountains.

* * *Althea* *

Flashes of lightning seen above the horizon reminded her of happier times in the market watching the temporary fires and flashes from magician's tricks.

The campfire served as the dividing line between the four snoring Long Bow Knights on one side, herself on the other. Oscar stood with his back to the fire. She watched him move around it squinting into the darkness.

* * *

Darkness covered the sky. The queen's eyes slowly opened. She stretched, and looked to the west. A slow, gentle rain moved in a third time, freshened the air, and dampened their clothes. She draped her coat on her head, and hoped her tight muscles would loosen as they hiked. "When will we break camp?" the queen asked.

"You are awake early," Oscar whispered, poking at the fire. "In about half an hour I will wake them. We will be ready at dawn. Go back to sleep."

"I cannot. My dream scared me."

"What happened?" Oscar asked.

"Please do not laugh," Althea began. She rubbed the red flat stone from her coat pocket. "I went to market and the archbishop had a merchant's cart selling arrows and knives. Bettina ran through the market. She had stolen a

228

knife and scabbard. *Family* had been carved in the leather."

"Have you seen Kendrick's knife?"

"No."

"Go on."

"Bettina chased me through the market. Merchants yelled as I ran by. They yelled, *You should not have slapped him. You should have never have told him you didn't want to see him.*"

"Not to worry, your majesty, I believe my son's sense of responsibility will come to your rescue regardless of your dream." He smiled.

"You are kind to say, but my sense of Kendrick is he will respect my wish over his own personal desires. You have raised the perfect gentleman. I have to seek him out and apologize. I believe there is a limited time for me, and then he will be off *chasing dragons*. You and I may never see him again."

"You may be right," Oscar replied, smiling, "but try not to worry. We should get going. We need to travel faster than Kendrick if we are to catch him. This is not going to be a pleasant day. Are you sure you want to go with us?"

"I am going."

"Yes, my queen."

* * *Kendrick* * *

Before dawn Kendrick prepared to climb the rocky butte. Today would be used for planning his dragon quest.

He ate the rest of the rabbit from last night's dinner and rearranged the weapons on his belt for speed of use. Satisfied, he fastened the belt on his waist. Taking a deep breath, he began his hike toward the butte.

A loud clattering noise came from the wooden soles he'd tied to this boots. Beads of sweat had already formed on his brow as he alternated between watching the sky and removing the noisy soles. Every second his nerves were elevated to another level. He decided to store the wooden soles in his bag.

It struck him that from here to the butte he had no cover; he was entirely visible from the sky. He felt like a rodent with a hawk circling above, except he did not have a hole to escape into.

The early morning shadows stretched out across the rugged landscape. Kendrick thought he could use these shadows when the time came and studied the area, determining a path that would give him the greatest chance of success. The first wedge pointed toward the first area of shadows.

The first screech of the day startled Kendrick. He ran to the shadows and bent down behind a high rock wall. The crouching dragon waddled out of the cave and stood on the edge of the rock cliff. While yawning and extending its wings, Kendrick's shoulders tightened; his knuckles turned white from gripping his bow wrapped over his shoulder.

It's big!

The dragon leaned forward and took flight. A few flaps increased its altitude and speed. It circled around the perch twice and flew directly overhead. Kendrick concluded the beast's wings were strong because they propelled that large body so easily. He couldn't risk a frontal attack—those powerful wings could swat him like a fly.

For over an hour Kendrick worked to find the best way through, over and around the uneven rocky terrain, his palms and fingertips tenderized from the steady gripping and leaning on the rock surfaces. He took a moment to rub his hands together hoping it would ease the stinging. The sky went dark for an instant. The dragon returned to the cave with a young calf head hanging from its mouth.

* * *Althea* * *

The early sun warmed her face as they walked. Althea walked behind Oscar attempting to step in the same spots as much as possible. The four Long Bows, following on her heels, were breathing heavily.

"This pace is challenging," one of the Long Bows whispered.

A sudden stop from Oscar caused an abrupt stop from Althea.

Two large fallen trees formed a "V" shape on the ground. Next to the larger tree the grass was matted. A yard away sat the fire rings encircling the charred wood.

"Here is where Kendrick spent a night." He pointed to the campfire.

"How can you be sure?" a Long Bow asked.

"Only Kendrick would take the time to put two rock rings around the fire. And we have been following his tracks," Oscar replied. "He is two days ahead of us."

"How can you tell he is two days ahead of us by merely looking at the campsite?" Althea asked.

"Simple math, no signs to read," Oscar replied. "At the coronation, Reginald said Kendrick had left the day before." He winked at her and then announced to everyone, "We will rest for a few minutes before we proceed."

The Long Bows sat on one side of the "V," Queen Althea sat on the other side, and Oscar walked around searching for tracks from Kendrick. He wandered away for about three minutes then returned.

"All right, we can continue. We are catching up. He's limping."

"How do you know?" asked one of the Long Bows.

"One footprint is deeper in the soil and it is the same side that has a smaller gait," Oscar replied. "I am worried that my son will be unable to fight the dragon with only one good leg."

* * Kendrick * *

The dragon softly landed on the ledge in front of the cave. It stooped to enter.

Kendrick waited for five minutes in case the dragon returned to the perch. He left a wedge and moved to the next patch of shadows. The shorter shadows limited his options, but he managed to find three suitable places to hide when the dragon flew overhead.

A quick look from behind showed he had covered about three quarters of the total distance. Kendrick ate some pine nuts and berries he'd picked before leaving the forest. It would soon be mid-afternoon and the shadows would disappear. He looked for an area with an overhang. None could be found. His option was to gamble that he could cross the flat area without being spotted by the dragon. He decided to run toward the closer front of the butte.

The uneven terrain and variable distances of the high points made his legs ache from the jarring rocks, and reminded him of the log jumble at the knight games. The concentration requirements created a slight headache. Fifteen minutes later he'd touched the base of the butte—sixty feet below the perch. Pain shot through his body; rubbing the thigh wound through his pants only increased the pain.

The gravel below the perch made it impossible to hide against the front base of the butte. Suddenly, a handful of gravel trickled onto the pile. The dragon appeared to be a giant disfigured bird.

Ominous!

Kendrick's feet would not move. It was as though they were frozen to the ground. Tense shoulders sent a sharp pain down his spine. Time slowed for several seconds. *Had he tackled something larger than his skills? Did he require additional help?* A few more gravel pieces fell, and the snap as they hit the pile awakened Kendrick from his temporary fog.

Slowly, he walked with shaky legs around the edge of the gravel to the side of the cliff. When the dragon screeched Kendrick froze. Had he been detected?

The dragon leaned over the edge and took flight. Red dominated his body and wing color with the exception of brown around the leg joints. Dark red stains began at the chin, skipped the neck, and continued onto the chest, probably from carrying dead animals. Two nostrils raised above the long flat face. A set of horns adorned the head like a crown. The fangs were long and black.

The dragon circled the butte twice and then flew away to the east. *That's odd. Why east?*

If the dragon happened to be a creature of habit, Kendrick had two hours to complete his objectives. He climbed the cliff below the perch, his tired fingers shaking from the tension from gripping the cliff's face.

When he reached the perch, he gagged as the strong stench of dead animals filled his lungs. The flat area in front of the cave's opening was surprisingly large. Approaching the cave opening, the smell continued to grow. Tying a rag around his nose and mouth, Kendrick thought it good he did not have large dragon nostrils that could inhale more sour air.

Inside the huge cave he found small animals, chickens, and large fish stuffed into the cracks of the walls, a near twenty-foot high pile of skulls and bones, and a large gravel area where he assumed the dragon slept. Maybe he should attack then? To his surprise the walls didn't have any burned areas.

Several stalagmites formed under the lines of dripping water and created a jail with a large open empty space behind. He discovered the slick, wet floor that surrounded the barrier when he slipped passing between two stalagmites.

He paced each area to determine its size. Satisfied he had an image of the inside of the cave, he returned to the opening.

Outside, off in the distance, he could see the dragon returning. Kendrick knew it would arrive before he could disappear over the cliff. He returned to the cave and hid behind the bone pile. The dragon had returned early.

The dragon landed softly. It stooped over, then shuffled into the cave and stuffed two large fish in a crack. The dragon sniffed the air and tilted its head as it looked toward the gravel bed. The beast continued to sniff and moved toward the bone pile.

Kendrick backed away. The dragon shuffled around the other side. Its eerie yellow eyes haunted Kendrick, reminding him of a few scary encounters he'd had with large barn owls. When the dragon reached the lowest part of the ceiling, Kendrick thought the beast would have a difficult time backing out. He ran out of the opening and climbed the large boulders along the eastside. He waited. The dragon never showed. Kendrick repelled down the back of the butte and left the rope. Running at full speed, he'd probably not make it back to camp before sunset.

* * *Althea* * *

"There it is," Oscar said.

"What? I do not see anything," Althea replied.

"Kendrick's second camp. Rest a few minutes."

Althea removed her hat and wiped the sweat from her forehead on her shirtsleeve.

"Thank you. I am tired. How far ahead is he?"

"Less than a day. We are not catching up as I expected," Oscar said. "We have another couple of hours before sunset." Althea followed Oscar's gaze to the woodchips on the ground near a fallen tree. "I wonder what he carved."

After resting, the weary team trudged along in silence.

The bottom of the sun touched the horizon as orange, pink, and purple painted the clouds.

"You men gather some firewood and find us some food."

"Do you think we will catch him?" Althea asked.

"It could be close. Hopefully, he has determined the size of his task. I hope he will take a day or two to plan," Oscar replied.

"Do the signs indicate anything different from yesterday?"

"Yes. His leg is getting worse. His gait is closer."

Two Long Bows returned with firewood and started the campfire. A minute later another brought two rabbits. Soon after, the last man arrived with wood.

As they put extra fabric in boots to cushion against the hard rocks and waited somewhat impatiently for the rabbits to cook, the dinner conversation turned to sore feet and how to gain time by cutting across the rocky flat area.

The four knights slept. She watched Oscar remove his hat and slowly run his hands over his head as he looked at the ground. Althea assumed that Kendrick's wellbeing was foremost in his mind.

* * *

Again she woke before the Long Bows. Oscar napped a few feet away. The cool autumn morning made Althea wish for an extra cloak or a blanket. Next to her lay two carved wood ovals and rope pieces. She wondered what they were.

"You strap them on your boots." Oscar said. He yawned. "Be ready to go in ten minutes. Divide up the food, we will eat while we walk."

* * Bettina * *

The cold pre-dawn air felt sharp to her skin. Winter was attempting to cut through the autumn frost; each expired breath from her lips turned to a burst of warm steam. Tugging at the hat, yanking the collar, then pulling the gloves trying to cover another tiny section of exposed skin, she contemplated tearing her dress sleeves to make a scarf to protect her ears.

At that moment she considered her education a waste. She did not know how to make a fire, hunt, cook, or ride a horse. She should have stopped at the site with the two-ringed campfire. Maybe she would be warmer knowing that a fire had existed there once.

Bright spots appeared in the trees then temporarily vanished. She felt small wisps of air touch her face followed by the slap of wings.

Focus. Bettina, focus!

The stars gave her peace from the hoots, skittering, howling, and scraping of her fifth night outdoors. Every night they gave her light and a canvas. She painted the spaces and gaps with her imagination—people she knew, places to visit, and the house she would own as soon as this task was completed.

Soon important people would name a constellation after her, Bettina Smythe. After all, the important ancients had their named stars. Her story would be in books and scholars would expound on her position in history. Even the poor would appreciate her removing the oppressive king and those who would continue his legacy.

Dragon's Castle

* * Kendrick * *

Awakened by the twitch from his painful thigh, Kendrick gently rubbed the wound. His muscles and joints ached from the strenuous hike to get here, and sleeping on the ground had been no picnic. He'd managed several falls during last night's return from the butte, but today he could rest his body, eat, and strategize on how to rid Manshire of its invader from the east.

Kendrick stretched and walked around for a few minutes to loosen up his body. For the first time, he wondered if he faced the same disease as his mother. *At his age, should he be having such difficulty with his joints?*

A sudden rush shot through his muscles and his shaky hands reached for his temples. Uncertainty and doubt snowballed, making him aware of his small size compared to that of the dragon. Rapidly, sweat formed on his forehead, palms, and shoulders as he thought about his limited dragon knowledge, his painful stiffening leg, and his limited weapons.

Father had taught him to focus and break projects up into tasks when confronted with doubt or a difficult situation. He thought through his options—not fighting the dragon, challenging the dragon at a later time, or taking on the dragon now. His nerves settled when he remembered that today existed for planning. He would make the final decision tonight.

For now he needed to eat.

His mother's scrambled egg omelet came to his mind—a mixture of many small things that had made the whole omelet delicious. Peppers added a unique acidic flavor. Spinach provided a rich unusual texture. Milk made the entire omelet fluffy. An assortment of beans enhanced the flavor. Like the ingredients of an omelet, his successful journey would be the result of blending the small tasks.

While eating his meal of pheasant and berries, he thought about the dragon. What were the weaknesses of such a large creature? He suspected that the dragon would be slow because it would take a lot of strength to move his large body—validated by the slow movements experienced at the bone pile.

It was a creature of flight—hadn't Reginald said it had had trouble moving about on the ground? It would have limited experiences with a prepared human being that its previous encounters were confrontations by surprised defenseless farmers. With no natural predators, it would be a creature of habit, and predictable behavior favored a surprise attack.

Searching the forest for long straight limbs and long oval rocks, he thought about Althea, a farmer's daughter whom fate had transformed into a princess. Her role had put her in many difficult situations, but these same challenges had only made her stronger. She'd even endured the near tragic Knight Games. Her life was surely destined for greater things.

He thought about his own life. Born a farmer knight's son who needed to be taught survival skills at an early age so he could care for his mother, the market *sheriff* role he thought would be his path to the Long Bows, had nearly resulted in his death. He had even served as the princess's confidant for a while. Now he'd started this dragon quest. Could his life be destined to complete one odd task after another?

A movement on the butte caught his eye—the dragon exited the cave and sat on the rock perch facing the sun. The perch stood three feet above the flat area and thirty feet from the cave opening. The dragon's feet rested on the one-foot wide wall. Its talons hung over the edges. A few minutes later the dragon stretched, leaned forward, and took flight.

As it disappeared over the horizon, Kendrick knew the dragon would destroy another family's home.

The dragon must be stopped.

Finding the poles, he then retrieved the flint he'd collected along the trail to make two spears, a club, and two fat shaft arrows. Kendrick chipped the triangular flint edges, split the end of the spear shaft, positioned the spearhead, and tied it in place with leather from the saddle armor. The same process produced the fat shafted arrows. The pheasant feathers were used for arrow fletching.

Kendrick pealed a square section of bark from a tree and used it to practice with his new weapons. The first spear toss missed the target and the second struck two feet below it. Shooting the two reinforced arrows turned out much better. Adjusting for their extra weight, the first arrow hit the tree about an inch above the target, and the second arrow, almost at the center of the square. He gathered the spears and arrows and continued to practice.

The dragon returned from its afternoon trip for the day.

Kendrick finished the pheasant, found a place to see the sunset, and started a fire. Rolling up his sack for a pillow, he went to sleep.

* * *Althea* * *

Midmorning, they came upon a large grey and tan boulder wedged between cliffs. Water sprung from its edges.

"There." Oscar pointed. "He went up there."

Oscar went first, helping Althea over the difficult terrain. She stretched to take a large step forward and progressed a few inches as the gravel easily shifted.

At the top of the short climb, Althea sat on a rock while Oscar walked around the small pond.

"He has been here and has stayed quite a while. This is good. We can close the gap between us."

"Any idea how long?"

"He swam then rested over there—maybe two to three hours. If we press hard we can get to half a day behind."

Trusting Oscar's judgment challenged her sense of reason. Rest would be a nice gift, but she understood Oscar's drive. He was not taking any chances with his son's life.

She slumped to the ground and slowly rubbed her puffy hands over her thighs. Occasionally, a severe pain, like a thorn in a boot, shot through the small of her back. But she would fight through the pain to find Kendrick.

The four Long Bows drank water from the pond.

"We can rest for ten minutes," Oscar said. "How is everyone? Do we think a slow run is possible?"

The Long Bows glanced at each other. One was about to speak when the queen said, "I can manage it."

She winked at Oscar knowing they would not let a girl beat them.

A few hours later they came across another of Kendrick's camps. Oscar checked the camp quickly then continued to lead the group.

The Long Bows were grumbling amongst themselves about the pace and their sore bodies.

"How can he keep up such a demanding pace?"

"Does he ever stop long enough to rest his legs?"

"Hopefully the queen will order a reasonable rest."

The queen heard them, and a quiet smile gave away her thoughts.

The sun's bottom edge touched the horizon as Oscar watched the butte in the distance.

"We will stop here for the night," Oscar said.

* * *Kendrick* * *

With his thigh wound throbbing and swollen tight against his pant leg, Kendrick awoke. He longed for the refreshing pond.

He checked the eastern horizon—it was early dawn.

Today was the day. Kendrick's journey, aches, pains, planning, and new weapons had become the total of his best effort to slay the dragon. Today, he would save his fellow countrymen from the *invaders from the north*. If he failed, Father would be ridiculed because his son would be perceived as not having any skill. He couldn't turn back now.

More pheasant and berries for breakfast filled his stomach while some were stored in his bag for later. He collected his new weapons and he ran as fast as his thigh would permit. In a mile he'd created a little extra time within the pockets of shadows, arriving twenty minutes ahead of the day previous.

The empty perch became visible in the early morning sun.

Kendrick found his marker and limped to the first shadowed location. His heartbeat quickened as he hiked, although he felt safer with the extra weapons. He waited a few minutes. No dragon. The marker pointed the way to the next location.

Kendrick hobbled to the next shadow pool. Nearing, the dragon appeared on the perch. The movement startled

Kendrick. Seconds later, he realized he'd dropped a spear. He stopped, backtracked, and retrieved it.

The dragon yawned showing it blackened teeth and tongue. Kendrick had another four minutes to the third location.

Once there, crouching in the shadow of the wall, his thigh felt like a torch. He would wait for the dragon to fly off before crossing the open flat area.

The dragon stretched its wings, leaned over the perch, and circled the butte twice before flying to the west. Kendrick gathered his things and limped for fifteen minutes to the rear of the butte. He tied the bag with all his weapons to the rope.

At the top his focus was fuzzy, his balance unsure. He glanced at the ground and found a place to sit. With closed eyes, he sat for a few moments pressing his palms above his temples.

Moments later, his focus had returned. He flexed his hands several times before lifting his weapons along the cliff. He carried everything to the spot he'd selected the day before. The spears were laid on the ground suspended between two small ridges, the club placed with the handle up leaning against the front ledge.

Surprised he had only one fat shaft arrow, Kendrick walked back to the edge and looked over the side—the other fat shaft arrow wasn't below. He returned to the weapons cache, removed his sword from the belt, laid it behind the front ridge, sat with his back against the ridge, and closed his eyes.

A red stain glistened on Pegasus' pure white hair from his right thigh.

He glanced down at it—a small orange fire burned on his pant leg.

Pushing his hand on the fire, it remained lit and would not be extinguished.

Time was running out to save Althea from Bettina.

He placed his palms above his temples to clear his thinking.

If he jumped onto Draco he could fight Bettina hand-to-hand.

He directed Pegasus to fly over Draco and then stood on Pegasus's back.

He turned to Althea and gave her the reins.

Kendrick jumped into mid-air.

His heart skipped a couple of beats as he felt the enveloping rush of energy.

Landing on Draco the dragon, he pulled the sword from his belt, raising it high above his head, the sword positioned to strike Bettina.

He was swinging the sword when suddenly, with a crack, Draco's tail bashed into his knees.

Kendrick fell, the rocky butte rapidly approaching.

Awakened by screech of the incoming dragon, Kendrick peered over the ridge. The dragon appeared to be angry; he'd returned without food. The beast's high-pitched screech was the loudest so far, forcing Kendrick to cover his ears, close his eyes, and lower his head.

His heart rhythm rapidly increasing, he rubbed his sweaty palms on his pants and suppressed a cry of pain when his hand brushed the wound.

For the first time in Kendrick's recollection, the dragon landed with a thud. Kendrick quietly approached the edge and looked down at the dragon's back.

243

The dragon was just ten feet below, picking up basket-sized stones with its feet and tossing them to the other side of the landing.

* Althea *

Oscar stopped suddenly, held up his hand, and whispered, "Quiet!"

Everyone heard it—a faint screeching noise.

Another screech. Much closer.

"There!" one of the Long Bows said. He pointed to the sky.

"Flaming dragons, he is big," Althea heard Oscar say under his breath.

Oscar broke into a run. Althea tried to follow but could not keep up. Two Long Bows passed her and two followed about ten feet behind. Althea gave up trying to catch up. She sat for a few minutes before Oscar returned.

"I think I saw him," Oscar declared.

"*Him* being Kendrick?" Queen Althea asked.

"Yes."

"Where?"

"On the same rocky butte where the dragon landed."

Althea placed her hands behind the small of her back and walked in a circle. *Kendrick was near the dragon?* "How far out?"

"Half to a full hour."

Excited about the sighting of Kendrick, but worried for him, it required only a moment for her energy to be renewed. A lingering smile revealed her delight. Time had stopped. She heard the branches of the pine trees rubbing together in the breeze, her back pain subsided, and her legs stopped aching. Just as quickly, her thoughts were jerked back to the trail.

"We should go," two Long Bows said.

"Are you all right?" Oscar asked her.

"Yes. Slightly winded, but I will be fine," she replied.

The four knights stood and nodded to Oscar.

Oscar paced his running to conserve energy. A mile from the forest's edge he stopped and pointed to a blackened area circled by two rows of rocks.

"He stayed here two nights," Oscar said. "We can rest later. We must carry on."

Oscar ran again. A few minutes later, he slowed to a fast walk and scanned the ground in earnest.

"What are you looking for?" Althea asked, breathing heavily.

"A wood wedge. I taught Kendrick to use well-placed wooden wedges to point to the next trap. This rock field would be a dangerous area to cross. Kendrick would need to find a way through, which would make him invisible to the dragon," Oscar replied.

"Is that what we are looking for?" Althea pointed to a triangle of wood sitting on a flat rock at the forest's edge.

"Yes," Oscar replied. Althea detected an excitement in Oscar's voice.

"How are all six of us going to cross this area?" asked one of the Long Bows.

"Only three are going across, and two will stay with the queen," Oscar said. He turned to Althea. "I must insist Queen Althea. I have not fought a dragon in my lifetime and I cannot be worried about you in a volatile, reactive environment."

Sad eyes revealed her understanding.

* * *Kendrick* * *

Slowly and quietly, like a praying mantis, Kendrick had positioned himself above the cave opening. He expected the dragon to come out soon for its afternoon flight. It had been quite a while since lowering himself between the two narrow rocky points above the cave opening.

His right leg had gone numb shortly after he'd sat to wait, though his left had just started to numb. He was thankful. Without pain he could focus on the task before him.

He lowered his head and closed his eyes. Strangely, he was at peace.

The screech startled him.

The dragon shuffled out of the cave. It stood erect as it cleared the opening. He only had a moment before the dragon took flight.

With an instant awareness that this was *his* moment, Kendrick looked down at the dragon's back, sudden sweat stinging his eyes. He adjusted the long bow and quiver for his jump. His knuckles were white as he gripped a spear in one hand and a sword in the other.

Taking a deep breath and thinking only of Althea, he leapt onto the dragon's back.

Whoosh! The dragon twisted and arched its back, slamming Kendrick into the cliff above. Kendrick groaned as the pain vibrated within his shoulders. He bit his lower lip. The dragon leaned forward; Kendrick could not endure another slam against the wall.

Thrusting the spear into the dragon's back, the beast screeched. *Was the shaft strong enough?* The beast quickly raised, pressing Kendrick against its large body, causing the spear to bend and break. It traveled even deeper into the dragon's flesh, but kept Kendrick from another slamming into the cliff.

Kendrick's ears were ringing, but something in the loud screeches penetrated his soul like a puppy not understanding his master's voice. The beast's neck scales felt slick like pond moss, and Kendrick struggled to hold onto the sword and remain on the dragon's back.

Using the exposed spear as a foothold, Kendrick pushed closer to the head. He wrapped his legs around the dragon's neck like riding a horse and leaned back to plunge the sword into its skull.

The dragon took flight.

It made a sharp right turn. Kendrick could see the ground formerly beneath the wing. Suddenly, the dragon turned. He could now see the ground under the other wing. He caught a glimpse of three men running across the rocky field but decided they were merely hallucinations. Before he could get a good look the dragon changed directions.

* * *Althea* * *

"*Kendrick!*" She pointed toward the dragon.

Oscar ran across the open rocky field then suddenly stopped. He picked up a stick. In that same instant two arrows pierced the sky toward the low flying dragon. Both Long Bow arrows bounced off the thick scales. Oscar was now close enough for Althea to see it wasn't a stick. He drew the bow past his cheek and aimed the thick-shafted arrow. Suddenly the tension on his bow was released. He held the arrow in his hand and ran.

The dragon's speed seemed to be increasing.

"What is he doing?" Althea asked aloud, not expecting a reply.

"The target is moving too fast. We could hit Kendrick," said one knight.

Althea placed her hands on her face, looked to her knights, glanced at Oscar, then fixed her gaze on Kendrick. As his sword thrust into the back of the dragon's head, the dragon screeched. It flew steeply upward. Kendrick hugged the dragon's neck as it dove toward the ground. The dragon's body twisted as his flight lowered within the sky.

Kendrick removed his sword and with one quick movement, drove his sword once more into the dragon's head.

247

The dragon screeched and turned back toward the cave.

Kendrick grabbed at several scales on the beast's back. The wings went still and then into a "V" shape, the back legs dropping as the body gradually shifted upright. Kendrick's hands flew from the dragon's back and it looked like he was rubbing something off his hands. The dragon landed hard in the rocky, flat area jarring Kendrick from its back.

She gasped as Kendrick's head struck a boulder. He lay motionless. She could not contain herself.

Seconds later a hand pulled her to a stop. "*Flaming dragons!* You dare to stop me?"

"My queen, Oscar threatened us if you left that spot," one of the Long Bows said.

"I am the queen. You serve to protect me. I am going to Kendrick."

Oscar raced toward the dragon—bow in one hand and an unusual arrow in the other. The dragon stumbled toward Oscar and then just as suddenly, stopped.

Kendrick sat, chin in his chest. He attempted to stand, but his balance was unsteady. He drifted uncontrollably to his right, placing his hands on the rock wall to steady himself.

Althea had crossed a quarter of the distance to Kendrick when she saw Oscar kneeling, loading the thick arrow, and pulling the string past his cheek.

She stopped and watched helplessly. Had Oscar knelt too far away? Had her presence created problems? She had no skills to help battle the dragon, and the two Long Bows assigned to protect her were restricted from fighting.

Kendrick staggered back toward the rock he'd struck when he'd fallen from the dragon's back. A crackling *whoosh!* caught everyone's attention. A huge fireball, the size of a water barrel was suddenly spit from deep within the dragon's throat, toward Oscar.

Oscar released the arrow then stretched out on the ground. He could feel the heat as the fireball flew over him.

The arrow struck the dragon in the left arm joint.

Angered screeching filled the air once more as the dragon turned away from Oscar. It blinked at Althea and her two knights standing in the rocky flat. It's angry eyes fixed on Althea.

She saw the dragon's teeth—all of them.

She could not even blink.

But the dragon's loud screech had quickly reduced to a whimpered groan. A puff of gray smoke flew from the dragon's mouth. He fell to its left, the fat shafted arrow sticking in a small hole behind its jaw.

"Kendrick!"

Suddenly his knees buckled, his limp body falling to the ground.

ANDEAN WHITE

Relentless Revenge

Oscar arrived at Kendrick's side before Althea. He checked Kendrick's breathing and extended his arms and legs for other injuries. When he touched his son's right thigh, Kendrick groaned.

Oscar carefully tore open the pant leg. The wound's outer crimson color blended to purple then light brown with a yellowish jelly oozing from the black center. He checked Kendrick's head. An inch cut had soaked his hair. Oscar tore off his own shirt sleeve and ripped it into two long pieces. One, he folded and pressed on the wound, the other, he tied around his boy's chin and wound.

He glanced as Althea arrived.

"How is he?" Althea asked in-between gasps of air.

Kendrick legs, hands, and arms were shaking.

"He is exhausted and his wounds are serious. The head is bleeding...and the thigh wound is infected. We might have to...cut off the leg," he struggled to reply.

Without hesitation, Althea said to the two Long Bows protecting her, "Go and find two long and strong poles, and ten shorter ones about three feet long. We shall make a stretcher to carry him out." She turned her attention to Oscar, "Are you all right?"

"Yes, fine."

Oscar held Kendrick's head level. It slowed the bleeding. Althea knelt and held Kendrick's rough, callused hand. Tears slowly rolled down her cheeks. "Kendrick, please forgive me for slapping you. I acted selfishly. Once again, you have saved my life. You are my good luck charm. I need you to protect me." She looked to Oscar. He nodded.

* * *Althea* *

During the assembly of the stretcher, Althea could feel she was being watched. Upon completion, they carefully placed Kendrick on the portable bed. A knight was on each corner.

They passed the last campsite and continued to the next. Kendrick groaned when the stretcher touched the ground. Oscar checked his son's wounds and then ripped off his other sleeve to replace the bandage.

"How is he?" Althea asked, still feeling as if something was penetrating her very skin. Was the dragon still alive?

"His fever is higher. The head wound isn't bleeding, but it is going to be tender," Oscar replied. "I hope we can save his leg."

"We have shared many head wounds—at the market, the big oak, the Knight Games, and now this. In a strange way, I hope this isn't the last one." She turned away and wiped at her eyes. But the presence was still there, almost breathing beside her.

She stood, looked at Kendrick, slowly walked to a fallen tree, and knelt with her fingers entwined: *Lord, my actions were selfish. If I'd kept my adoption misgivings from him, Kendrick would not be so close to death. Please do not punish him for my mistake and thoughtlessness. He is a good man, and we need him...I need him. If it be your will, please let him live. Amen.*

As she stood it was if the trees were speaking to her. What was it that she was feeling? Why did her heart beat so, and her skin burn with fear? She searched the horizon for the beast, but he was surely dead...

* * *

Neither Althea nor Oscar slept.

At dawn, Oscar woke the Long Bows.

Kendrick groaned, his eyes opening then closing.

"Kendrick, can you hear me?" Althea asked. He was silent and his shallow breathing concerned her.

"Pond," Kendrick whispered.

"What did he say?" Oscar asked.

"Pond," she answered.

"We passed the pond on the way up," Oscar said. "Remember? Kendrick spent a lot of time there. He must have perceived a benefit other than simply quenching his thirst; otherwise, he would have walked by it. He is like me in that regard, driven to complete a task. Hurry!"

* * *

Althea stood, pressing her palms in the small of her back. The pain shooting up her spine while bending to clear rocks and limbs for the Long Bows carrying Kendrick was almost unbearable. But she would do it.

By late evening they had all arrived at the pond. Kendrick woke for a few seconds, groaning, his head rolling to the side. And then he must have seen her because a half smile appeared on his face.

Oscar removed Kendrick's shirt and boots. Two knights helped ease Kendrick into the pond. Oscar waded in the water to support him then instructed the four Long Bows to build two narrow rafts.

Kendrick's eyes opened. He smiled at Oscar.

"You are going to be healed, son," Oscar said.

The knights took several minutes to collect fallen logs and lash them together. Oscar ordered them to make a net and tie it between the two rafts. He placed Kendrick in the net—his body under water except for his face.

"My hips, knees, and feet are feeling better. The yellowish jelly has disappeared from Kendrick's wound, and his hands are healing from the climbing," Oscar said.

"Do you think this is healing water?" Althea asked.

"Might be. Abbey could have used this."

"Abbey?"

"Kendrick's mother. She had a joint affliction that finally took her life. Kendrick cared for her from an early age."

Althea glanced at Kendrick then back at Oscar. She considered his son's commitment to care for his mother and the farm from his youth. She looked at the father that appeared to be standing taller, and whispering to his son. Her smile was complete.

"We will be here for a few days. Build a fire, find some food, and gather some grasses or long pine needles for bedding," she told the knights.

Oscar gently pushed Kendrick to shore and stepped out of the water. He called one of the Long Bows over to collect some plants he'd seen around the pond.

"What are your plans?" Althea asked.

"This oily warm water appears to have healing properties. I am hoping to make a paste to stop the infection pulsing through his body. Maybe the paste will speed up his recovery."

"How can I help?"

"We need two bandages, a flat and round rock, and a flat stick."

* * *

Althea gathered the items. Oscar crushed the ingredients with the round rock. Three small piles of wild pumpkin leaves, linseed flax flowers, and ginger rested on the flat rock. Oscar carefully selected the whitest ash from the fire pit and made a fourth pile. He mixed the four piles together, scooped the mix into two pieces of

Althea's sleeve, and rolled the bandages. Wood slivers were woven into the ends to entrap the mixture.

"How did you learn to do this?" Althea asked.

"Abbey had a gift for using plants and other materials to help heal. She used to make a mixture to improve Kendrick's breathing in the spring, until he was eighteen."

Oscar slid into the pond, held Kendrick's head above the water, and tied the new rolled bandage over the wound. When Oscar laid Kendrick's head back into the net, the water bubbled. Following the same procedure, he dressed the thigh wound.

Kendrick groaned.

Althea placed the last stone for the campfire completing the two rings. She glanced over the pond and watched Oscar's head as it slowly fell to his chest, the next moment jerking upright. *Too many sleepless nights*, Althea thought, *and a father's worry had final caught up with him.* She walked to the pond's edge, still wondering about the fear in the air, or was it only within her own heart?

"Oscar, as your queen I am commanding you to rest," she said. "You are no good to us like this." She waived over to a knight. "Take Oscar's place."

"I am all right. This is my son. I need to care for him," Oscar said.

"I am the queen. And I care for Kendrick as much as you do, but we need your mind and skills to be sharp for all of us."

"Yes, my queen."

He walked over to where a Long Bow was sitting by the fire, placed his knife in his boot, and sat on a nearby log. He watched his son from a distance and fell asleep within a couple of minutes.

Althea motioned to the Long Bows to gather by the pond. "You two have the first detail of guard duty tonight," she said pointing at them directly and then to the knight in the pond. "We will take him out of the water in an hour, and place him on the stretcher to keep him off the ground. Gather some firewood before sleeping. When it is time, take second guard detail."

* * Bettina * *

Her anger had been growing since she'd lost the tracks miles earlier, but now her luck had returned. Had it not been for the screeching sound, and later, two Long Bows gathering wood, she would have missed the pond.

Bettina watched silently, following the group back to their camp. The near full moon lighted the night. She watched as Kendrick occasionally jerked and Althea touched his red face. Bettina would take care of him last. First, would be Stanley, Hunter's brother, the now rich, unreliable hired hand sleeping by the fire.

She was in luck yet again when three hours after dark, Stanley and another knight began separately patrolling the pond and adjacent forest area. Stanley seemed to be following someone. He'd made a big arc around the camp, and had suddenly slowed. Picking up a stone, he approached someone from behind, and with a quick movement, struck him at the top of the neck. He removed what appeared to be rope from inside his shirt and tied up the knight.

Bettina waited as Stanley finished. And then, quietly approaching him, she placed the sharp point of the knife against his back. He flinched and the point pierced the skin enough for a drop of blood to stain his shirt. He turned around slowly and Bettina's steady hand placed the knife against his chest. A drop of blood stained his shirt just below his breastbone.

Their eyes met. She saw the momentarily bulged eyes and heard him whisper "How did—", as she pressed the knife a tiny bit further, blood grew crimson as another few drops wet a line on his shirt below the blade.

"Bettina, I heard you were dead," the man gasped, holding his hands in the air.

"An exaggeration," she replied. "What is happening here?"

"Finally, I have the opportunity to execute the tasks you paid me for," Stanley replied. His tone faded as his gaze drifted from Bettina's eyes to his bloody shirt.

Suddenly, the knife she had thought to put away was at her throat.

She breathed heavily, thinking of death, of the destructive fire from her drawings.

Stanley smiled. "How did I do?" he asked.

She was surprised. "Thank you for the demonstration," she offered.

He continued to smile and removed the knife from her throat. "You are welcome. How did you get here?" He tore a piece of his sleeve and used it as a bandage.

"I have my ways. What is your intent with leaving this knight here?"

"He is a servant, an innocent pawn. I am here to avenge my brother's death at the hands of Oscar and Kendrick. The fact that I can also complete our agreement is purely coincidental."

"So you have a plan?"

Stanley put up his hand. He stared straight ahead.

"What is it?" she whispered.

He placed his index finger over his lips. Seconds later his shoulders relaxed and he looked at her. "Yes, I have a plan."

"As the financier of this raid, I want to know."

He rubbed his palm over his chin.

"All right. I will disable the other two Long Bow knights quietly as they sleep."

"How?" she interrupted.

"That is none of your concern. You paid me, and I will use methods that I am comfortable with," Stanley asserted. "That leaves an exhausted Oscar, his gravely ill son, and a young untrained queen."

"She is the queen?" Bettina's eyes widened.

"Yes, it has been a week now."

"Oh, I could not have planned this any better."

Stanley's quizzical expression was answered almost immediately.

"I get to remove a link in the chain of misfortune that has become my life," she said. Bettina walked in a haphazard circle rubbing her cold hands in delight. "Yes! Althea, you interrupted my uncle's plan to rid the king of an heir, ending the evil reign of king Louis's family."

"Who are you talking to?" Stanley asked.

"Sorry," she said softly, the fire within her increasing. "You *must* allow me to help. *I deserve* to be part of this moment." She watched his eyes widen and move away from her. "Sorry, please continue..."

Bettina watched the slight tilt of his head. She assumed he was uncomfortable with her. "I am your servant," she said. "Please continue with your scheme so I may support you."

He stroked his beard stubble.

"Truly, I am your servant," she whispered.

"I will awaken Althea first—she is the key to controlling Oscar. As much as I would like for Oscar to see his son die as revenge for my brother's death, I cannot risk Oscar's escape. The queen is next as she represents the next highest threat. Finally, Kendrick will be rolled into the pond where he will drown."

"Can I hold Althea while you take care of Oscar?" Bettina asked.

"Yes, but you must stay still and not give Oscar any edge. His skill is truly dangerous to us."

"I will hold his son's knife against Althea's throat until Oscar is no longer a threat. Leaving my uncle's handkerchief will make the searchers think a ghost did this."

"Agreed."

* * *

Bettina watched from behind a boulder. She waited for Althea to finally fall asleep. Leaving her observation post to report back to Stanley, a calming confidence filled her soul.

"They are asleep."

She followed him slowly and quietly to the campfire. One at a time, Stanley tied a knot in the middle of the short rope before he slid it around the Long Bows' throats. The knot was tied snuggly against the Adam's apple, allowing him to control the Long Bows like a harness on a horse. They were quiet as he tied them up.

Bettina shook Althea's shoulder. Her eyes opened for an instant, closed, then opened fully. Bettina placed a finger against her lips, placed the knife against the queen's throat, and motioned Althea to get up.

The queen slowly stood.

With the queen secured, Stanley poked Oscar with the point of his sword. Oscar opened his eyes, followed the edge of the sword to Stanley's hand, and up the sleeve to Stanley's face.

Oscar glanced across the campfire. Althea was standing. The flickering fire reflected off the blade at her throat. Two Long Bows were tied and gagged.

"If anything happens to me before you die, Bettina will use your son's knife. We are going over by the spring. Stand, Oscar. Slowly."

It was sunrise and the long shadows cast an eerie pattern on the pond area.

"Oscar did you really think you could simply take my brother?" Stanley asked.

"Your brother died at his own hand," Oscar replied.

"My brother would never take his life!"

"He attacked a Long Bow while under custody. Hunter knew he had no chance of escape."

"Doesn't matter. Kneel as if you are praying to the healing properties of the spring."

* * Oscar * *

Before he turned away, Oscar glanced at Bettina who held Althea. He knelt, then listened for clues— the grass crunching under Stanley's feet as he walked backwards, the sword point being pushed into the ground, the arrow being removed from the quiver, the long bow being removed over the head, and Bettina moving Althea away from the campfire smoke.

He could feel the bow being stretched behind him and was grateful that Stanley had not found his knife, which now dangled in his hand.

He leaned to roll, when he heard the string snap and the sudden *whoosh!* of an arrow.

Another string snap caught his attention. This time it didn't miss but struck him in the lower left rib cage. He turned as Stanley fell face first to the ground.

Bettina turned.

Kendrick was standing in his underclothes holding Oscar's bow.

* * Kendrick * *

"Hello, Bettina. It's a shame you have to wear that rabbit coat. You deserve sable. I imagine you are hungry," Kendrick said. His heart pounded, his fear greater than it had been jumping on the dragon's back. He glanced at his father grimacing from pain.

"Not even a sable coat with matching hat and gloves will keep me from fulfilling my revenge," Bettina said as she moved Althea between herself and Kendrick.

260

"I will go fetch us some pheasants. Althea can keep the fire while you two discuss old times." Bettina exhaled and bit her lower lip. "Or, talk about the future," Kendrick added.

"I have waited too long to extract Uncle's and my revenge. We have been cheated out of our rightful place in the kingdom," Bettina argued. Her arm tensed as she watched over Althea like a dragon.

"I agree. The king stole your birthright. You were a young lady of society with fine clothes and many friends. Your world began to fall apart when your grandfather was appointed the Minister of Monetary Issues."

"I am in control here. Stop trying to trick me."

The knife moved slightly. A trickle of blood rolled down Althea's throat.

Kendrick's dropped the bow and arrow. He held his palms out for Bettina to see.

"This is not about control. You are perpetuating a battle that goes back many years before any of our births. Do any of us know where it actually started? Once you have killed us, how can you be sure it's the end? You have the opportunity for a great life."

He stopped speaking, allowing his thoughts to germinate within Bettina's mind.

"Think about the future. The queen gifts you money to start Bettina Smythes Artistry. Your success makes you a master. People pay you handsomely for portraits, landscapes, and murals. Your name and art lives forever through journals, books, and exhibits."

"You cannot make that happen," she argued.

"I just killed a dragon, survived an infected leg, and was healed by the love of family and friends near a warm water pond. I can do anything I set out to do." He glanced over to Althea's open mouth and focused stare. A tear rolled down each cheek. "Think of that, enjoyable dinner parties, friends, gifts, a mate, and a home—maybe children."

Bettina looked into the woods. She pulled Althea closer to her. "You are lying to me and making this up so I will drop this knife."

"Bettina, I have never lied to you. And I will use my influence with this queen to keep any promise I make to you." He smiled at Althea. "I have, after all, saved her life a few times."

"But that is your job."

"I was never in the king's employ."

Bettina held the knife slightly away from Althea's throat. As if she were looking for guidance, Bettina looked into the fire.

Althea's eyes looked from center to left several times, but she continued to say nothing.

Bettina nudged Althea. "Is this true?" she asked.

"It is true," Althea replied.

Bettina was silent. Her glazed stare returned to the fire. He saw the slight relaxation of the knife at Althea's throat.

"Bettina, think about the wonderful paintings you would not give the world. Right now, if each of us continues on the paths of our elders—you will kill the queen, Father will kill you with his knife, and I will be forced to kill Stanley to save my father."

Bettina looked at Oscar, moved the knife from Althea's throat, but continued to hold the blade over her shoulder.

Kendrick motioned with his hand and Althea stepped aside. An arrow's whisper escaped the sparse forest above the spring and struck Bettina below the back ribs. Bettina turned, gasping for air. The fourth Long Bow that Stanley had left tied in the woods was preparing another arrow.

Kendrick ran...

But he was too late. Just as the arrow pierced Bettina's upper back, she was caught by his hands.

* * *

Kendrick gathered Stanley's weapons and dumped the quiver on the ground. All the arrowheads were the same size as the shaft.

"Father, Stanley is alive, but not alert. He cannot tell us anything. The quiver contains only bodkin points. I suggest pulling it out."

Oscar grimaced.

"But first where did you learn that technique?"

"From you, at Hunter's interrogation," Kendrick said. "Here, bite on this stick."

Oscar smiled, bit the stick, then said, "Stop, stop."

"Kendrick, just yank it out. I'm feeling every little bump of the shaft," he said.

"On three. One, two..."

Kendrick removed the arrow with one quick pull.

Oscar yelled, then fell asleep. Althea dressed the wound with material from Bettina's dress.

The same procedure was performed on Stanley before his hands and legs were bound.

Bettina's body was covered with limbs from the leafy trees and buried next to the oldest pine. Though a small service might have been expected, not a word of sadness was spoken. For no one there had cared for Bettina, and her choices had finally ended her short life.

Throughout the rest of the morning, Kendrick and the Long Bows took turns holding Oscar and Stanley in the pond.

Although Kendrick's wounds continued to improve during his rotation, he grew tired by mid-day. Althea watched him stumble to the log where he sat with his elbows on his knees; his head to the ground.

Althea arrived a few minutes later. "Our two patients are improving. How are you?"

"I will be better after a little rest," Kendrick replied. He stood and offered his hand as she sat down. As he sat, he cherished the thoughts of their meetings at the market, the big oak tree, and the grand curve. He smiled at the joy these thoughts gave him. He faintly remembered an apology; he rubbed the back of his neck and thought of the slap.

Althea moved closer to him, she rubbed her thighs, then momentarily crossed her arms. She finally rested them on her knees.

"I am guessing you, Oscar, and Stanley will be well enough to travel in two days," she said.

During the silence between them, he looked at her and she turned to face him.

"Kendrick, I want to apologize again for slapping you. I am sorry."

Cupping her chin he rubbed the tears with his thumbs.

She continued, "And, I never should have said—"

He placed a finger on her lips. "We should not apologize for the past. We can learn from those moments to improve our future."

"We make a good team," she whispered.

"I had those same thoughts this morning," he replied.

Without prompts, both reached into their pockets and retrieved the red flat stones from the grand curve. They smiled and exchanged stones.

A soft breeze whisked though the clearing. The limbs of the small trees swayed and the leaves gentle rustling seemed to surround and separate them from the rest of the world.

"I love you," she said.

"I love you."

He leaned in anticipating their first kiss. Their foreheads bumped. After a few silent moments, they rubbed their foreheads and laughed.

An awkward moment followed, as he wasn't really sure what to do next.

Another breeze like a gentle hand nudged them closer together.

Kendrick touched her hair and she gently pressed her head against his hand. He placed his other hand along her cheek, gently touching her forehead. The scent of her hair filled him with an emotion he had never before felt. It was like heaven.

They looked into each other's eyes as their lips touched.

ANDEAN WHITE

Andean White

After family, Sage the dog, and biking, writing is my joy.

My career as a small business owner was cut short by Parkinson's Disease. After the decision to sell the business was made, it became apparent that few of the buyers knew how to develop a business plan. Writing an e-book on "How to Purchase a Small Business" seemed so logical. It was a good guide with lists of questions and a sample business plan. But marketing it became another matter.

A new hobby of writing travel journals, sprinkled with a little encouragement from family and friends, sparked a desire to test my writing skills, and decided it was time for that dream job—coffee on the deck, smokin' keyboard, e-books zooming through the Internet, and dollars collecting in the bank account.

Early spy short stories were posted on free e-book sites and developed a small following, which I thought was large enough to attempt a book. That second book was disappointing, but the experience was invaluable. And, I knew I wanted to write.

I fell back on my small business experience, and surrounded myself with the best people.

Two years later, I was an aspiring writer, telling stories that hopefully guide a reader's imagination to a world of excitement, and provide a brief rest from everyday duties.

I discovered that true writing was hard work, and quality required a lot of detail awareness. Maybe, there was still a chance of coffee on the deck...someday.

As a young boy at family gatherings, I recall listening to the men after a meal. The opinions around the subjects of politics, car brands, hippies, and rock n roll filled the room with energy like aromatic smoke from a pipe. But, when the story telling began everyone found a seat or patch of floor. We sat for hours laughing and gasping at the stories, fact or fiction—they shaped who we became and it strengthened our imaginations. Fifty years later, it's clear, a world without imagination would be pretty boring.

Marrying my high school sweetheart was my most brilliant accomplishment. We enjoy sporting events, backyard barbeques, outdoors, concerts, and traveling with our friends.

Winter's Thief is the first of a three book series, and it's available at the website www.AndeanWhite.com in soft cover and e-book. Also, find links to the top Internet bookstores.

Watch for Saraton Summer coming out in 2015.

Parkinson's Disease donation

1.0% to 1.5% of the population has Parkinson's disease—odds are someone on your street has Parkinson's.

Statistically, one, two, maybe three people on most major flights are affected with Parkinson's. A concert of 20,000 people will have 200 to 300 patients struggling daily with a disease that reveals itself in a long list of debilitating symptoms. The most visible is a shaking hand, chin, arm, leg, or foot.

20% of all profits will be donated to Parkinson's disease research.

ANDEAN WHITE